PREFACE

This book is a collection of short stories written over a period of forty years. Many of them have been published in magazines like *Candis* and *Cotswold Life*, others read on *BBC* radio or television, some were selections for *The Times* and *The Sunday Times* Cheltenham Literature Festival through *Gloucestershire Writers' Network*, or featured in anthology publications showcasing various British writers.

In compiling them I found several more that have never previously been in print, and are exclusive to this book!

It's such a thrill to have the opportunity to share them all with you. I really hope you enjoy reading them as much as I have enjoyed writing them over the years.

Ann

Let Me Tell You a Story

Ann Leyfield

Copyright © 2024 Ann Leyfield

All rights reserved.

ISBN: 9798873595952

First Edition. Edited & typeset by Samuel Victor for Victorious MCG © 2024

DEDICATION

I would like to thank all my family and friends who have encouraged me with my writing over the years. I've always loved telling stories and I feel very fortunate that there have been so many people willing to listen to them.

CONTENTS

ALL CHANGE

You Deserve Better	002
Six Mince Pies	005

A BIT OF A LAUGH

Olé Olé Olé	010
Just a Bit of Fun	013

AS TIME GOES BY

The Winds of Change	018
The Primrose Line	023
Remember the Welsh Doll	026
The Flag at Ranscombe Bay	031

WISHFUL THINKING

Sandy Shores	038
The Red Dress	041
Good Night George	045
Hands at the Window	048
Nearly Home	051
Your Day Will Come	055

GETTING TO KNOW YOU

Little Blue Number	062
Autumn Leaves	067
Thomas	069
The Jolly Man	071
Follow My Leader	076

A TIME AND PLACE

Gloucester's Child	082
One August Morning	084
Talbot Way	086

TALES OF THE UNEXPLAINED

The Six O'Clock Bus	090
A Song for Tilly	094
Molly's Shoes	098
Sweet Lillies of Easter	101
Deep Waters Run Still	105
To Pep You Up	108
The Daffodil Season	112

FROM A CHILD'S POINT OF VIEW

Josh	118
The Bookmark	122
Golden Sands to Grey	126
Ginnie	130
Gotta Read by Spring	137
The Wishing Stone	141

BING-BING STORIES

Victor Meets Bing-Bing	149
Bing-Bing and the Caravan	152
Bing-Bing and the Penguins	155

All Change

YOU DESERVE BETTER

It began when I answered the pay phone in the lobby.

"Gena, it's Frank. Don't hang up. I'm sorry about yesterday. I haven't got much time. Listen. At ten o'clock meet a man at the newspaper stall in Temple Meads Station. He'll be carrying a briefcase. You must say that the weather is beyond a joke and he'll give you the case. In the side pocket will be two airline tickets to Spain. Meet me at the airport at four with the case. Gena, you know I've always said that you deserve better. It'll be a new life for us. Got to go, the boss is coming…"

He hung up.

I slumped down to squat on my heels, the dead phone still in my hand. The cold from the damp frayed lino chilled my legs. Absent-mindedly I poked a finger through the hole in my slipper. He sounded so desperate. The problem was that I was not Gena, and I had no idea who she was. It must have been a wrong number.

I was alone in the house. The landlady was away and the other bedsit was empty. At that moment I needed someone to talk to, anyone would do. I should ring the police. It sounded as if he was part of some sort of crime. Anyway, money would be involved, a case full of money. I pulled my ragged dressing gown around me and left the cold lobby to return to my room.

Walls blotted with black damp seemed to watch me as I stared out at the rain through the yellowed net curtain. Another wet Monday, no job, no money and I'd run out of bread for toast. I kept hearing his voice repeating the words, "You deserve better… you deserve better."

"Yes I do!" I shouted. With a glance at the clock I knew if I hurried, I could make it to Temple Meads by ten.

I knew the station well. I had used it often when I had visited my parents, but that seemed years ago. I practised saying, "The weather is beyond a joke… the weather is beyond a joke." I said it over and over so as not to forget.

There were several men with cases on the platform. I started to panic, but remembering the squalor I had just left I gingerly walked to a man by the newspaper stand who had a briefcase by his side. The shop girl with peroxide frizz and red plastic earrings was serving him.

"What some awful weather," she said, "it's been raining for days, in fact it's no joke."

The man hesitated and picked up the case. I desperately interrupted and pronounced loudly, as if reciting some sort of creed, "In fact the weather is beyond a joke!"

Our eyes met.

"Are you Gena?"

I nodded stupidly. He gave me the case.

The shop girl started chewing gum and adjusting her tights. I smiled and quickly slipped away. Little did she know how close she had come to a fortune.

Who cared that the rain was dripping from my skirt down my bare legs? What's wrong with rain when you're rich?

I walked past the old church by my digs. Large words in black print shouted from the notice board. "We need £300,000 for the repair and renovation of the roof." I clutched the case harder and hurried on. The red placards at the Gas Board announced, "An offer you can't refuse" It was almost as if they knew.

Breathless, I arrived back, shut the door and tried to open the case. There were the airline tickets but the case itself was locked. Eventually I managed to force it open by cutting the leather strap. Inside were cloth money bags and some cheques made to *Warringtons*, the large store in town.

"Stolen money," I told myself, "but I'll be set up for life."

I packed madly, grabbing every worthless article I owned and pushing them into a dusty holdall. With the bag and case, I ran to the front door. A small white envelope was on the mat with a dark skinned bony face of a child staring at me with the message underneath, "Twenty pounds a year would save this child." He looked hopeful. I broke eye contact with the picture. *I deserve it!* Kicking it aside I opened the door to a young woman grasping a case.

"I've come for the spare bedsit."

Nervously, she smiled. "I was meant to come yesterday." She put out her hand to shake mine. "I'm Gena."

SIX MINCE PIES

"George Street is not what it was" – that's what I said when I saw them move into number 32, right opposite me. Then as the weeks went by I thought it was a good job that Mrs D wasn't there to see the state of her precious front step – not a dab of red polish now. And those curtains? Multi-coloured sunflowers!

The new woman went shopping at the corner shop, sometimes with a head scarf over her rollers. I'd seen her pop to buy a paper wearing slippers! Mr Jones from the shop told me once she came in for just one onion then decided to have some mushrooms as well. He'd laughed at her and said, "Do you want only one of them too?"

Every morning the new woman stood at her front door in a candlewick dressing gown for all to see as she waved to her husband going off to work. I thought he must have a job at the foundry. I'd seen him cycling home, grimy, with an open-neck shirt.

It was Christmas Eve when he came home with a tree tied to his bike. It had been a few years since Mrs D had put up a Christmas tree. We both never bothered. We just met up at three o'clock to hear the speech and raise a glass.

They were arranging the tree at the front window opposite. I remembered the one Tom and I had had when we were first married. We could only afford some cheap lights and then with a twinkle in his eye he'd taken out of his pocket a little wooden reindeer. He'd bought it at the corner shop and when he was tying it on the branch he said it was especially for me. I'd kept it all these years in my bedside drawer amongst my muddles and mementos. One antler was a little chipped and the dappled paint worn away but I decided to put it on the mantelpiece – my only decoration.

The two boys from opposite opened my front gate. They were scruffy little lads who kicked a ball about the street. I'd never spoken to any of them so I wondered why they were coming to see me. Then I guessed – not another lot! They were arguing in whispers as to who was going to knock at the door but I opened it quickly before they could and sharply said,

"If you've come carol singing I'm not interested. You must be the fourth bunch I've had this week!"

"No," said the older boy, "Mum sent these."

He handed me a small round cake tin and inside were six mince pies. They smelled delicious and were still warm. Well, I was so taken aback! – "her" from over there had sent these for me…

"Well you'd better come in," was all I could think to say. Their eyes looked everywhere, then the little one said:

"No trees… no decorations."

"Well you don't bother on your own," I snapped. "I'll get you a drink, sit down."

While I was in the kitchen I heard the older one say, "Now don't touch it. It's not ours."

When I came in I saw them looking at the reindeer.

"My husband gave me that nearly forty years ago," I whispered. They both smiled and I started to smile too. Then the older one pronounced,

"Mum said if you were on your own tomorrow you could come over and have a bit of dinner with us."

I was lost for words. I started stuttering badly.

"Well that's kind… more than kind, but I'll stay in my own as always. Thank her, mind you do…really kind."

As they were going I could see the little one looking back at the reindeer. I don't know what came over me but I grabbed it and put it in his hand, saying

"You have it. Put it on your tree." His eyes lit and he wished me "Happy Christmas." They both waved when they reached the door.

Alone now, the house was dull and I felt cold. Looking around the walls I thought I really hadn't bothered since I'd been on my own. I remembered the old box of trimmings in the spare room and decided I might as well get them out. As I was passing the front window I saw over the road a little hand fixing the reindeer on to the Christmas tree. He was taking great care to place it very close to the glass – where I could see it too.

A Bit of a Laugh

OLÉ OLÉ OLÉ

Picture it: Warm sand, the clear blue Med. Breeze rustling amongst the palm trees and here you are. What's your name? Well you are privileged to say, "My name is Andy – your *Sympson Sunshine Representative* to make sure you have the holiday you'll never forget! *Have a Sunshine day!*"

May I present you with your badge and your essential *Sympson* diary. You'll soon learn the two main golden rules: keep the punters busy and don't forget to smile!

Open your diary to the first page and I'll take you through a typical *Sympson Sunshine* day.

We pick them up at Gerona Airport at about 3 AM. They've had a long flight, they think they're tired, but once they've arrived at the *Hotel Marguerite* – we let them know their holiday has begun. Just a word of warning – some punters feel they should have a bed ready for them, but we say how much better to wait until 11 AM when their rooms will be actually empty.

You entice them into the all night bar for their welcome

drink of sangria. We then give them the low down for the week to come – trips, parties, discos and a typical *Sympson Sunshine* day. This is where you will see their enthusiasm soar with unbelieving expectation. So much is free – no extra cost. "Keep your euros in your pocket", as we say.

Yes lad, it's all written down ready for you in your diary.

The Typical Day:

- 6 AM *Sympson Sunshine* wake up call. All guests vacate their rooms by 7 AM for *Aqua-Stretch* by the pool with Ravey Davey.
- 8 AM Trampolining
- 9 AM Quiz time on *The Sombrero* Sun Terrace.
- 10 AM French Boules on the front lawn and the kiddies disappear to The *Tooty Owl* Club – free T-shirt, colouring and sticking galore.
- 11 AM Crazy golf with inflatable clubs, then…
- Noon Paella party by the pool with Flamenco dancing - we all have to show a leg – and finishing with the popular *Clap-a -Castanet* competition.
- 1 PM At leisure in your room – Siesta Time with recorded Basque bagpipe tunes (a bit of culture for the punters.)
- 4 PM Bingo in the main bar – winning numbers' prize could be a free half hour's roller-skating or bungee jumping in the Pyrenees.
- 5 PM Magic with *Uncle Pépé* and *Miguel the Master Bull* (Don't call him "tatty toro" in front of the kids.)
  Happy Hour for the oldies
  (beer and spirits are not included.)

7 PM   Evening Meal – alternating between fish, pork… different fish or, other fishy things…

8 PM   Disco Time. Oldies but goldies – Da Doo Ron Ron, sha lal lala lee and woe woah woah, to say nothing of *Viva España* and Olé Olé Olé…

By 10 PM some are beginning to flag, but you have your duty as a *Sympson Sunshine* representative to make the most of their time so it's *The Beach Party* – tennis; jump the waves competition; beach acrobats and then it's tuck into barbecued pork chops (pig's trotters to you and me!)

Then an opportunity for some genuine Catalan country dancing, (we tend to make them up as we go along.)

By 3 PM it's *Show Me the Way to go Home* as we *Conga* along the corridors bidding them "Buenos Noches" as we drop them off to snoozy land!

Well, it's non-stop but it makes it all worthwhile when they say it made them look at their hum-drum home lives in a totally new way. *Have a Sunshine day!*

JUST A BIT OF FUN

"There's no such thing as fibs – they're lies!"

My Mum told me that when I was little, but it all became a habit – just a bit of fun. It happens when I'm bored. Just like recently I was queuing at the Doctor's reception and I told the woman in front I had a terminal illness. She was so sorry she let me go in front of her.

At the bus stop I told an old man I'd just passed my degree with the *Open University*. I said I had to scrub floors for two years to pay the fees. He was most impressed.

On a dull morning when Jack had gone to work and I was collecting the bottles from the step, I told Erma, the mousey widow from next door, that the milkman and I were having an affair. You should have seen her eyes stretch when I whispered with a wicked grin, "Keep it under your hat, it's just a bit of fun on the side!"

I suppose marrying Jack had been the most sensible thing I'd ever done. He's solid, reliable – the sort of man who polishes his shoes when they're already clean.

He never goes out without crossing his scarf over his chest. Each night he sat in front of the television watching the news and documentaries. He loves those travel films. He once said that he was interested in what goes on in the world. Clearly not in my world – neither was I.

I was bored by it.

I saw the advert: "Good looking divorced man. Anxious to meet a lovely woman with a fun loving spirit."

I thought, "That's me!"

It was as if I'd found myself. With a flourish of perfumed paper I kissed the letter good luck as I posted my reply. He wrote back return of post. I hid the letter in my pinny pocket until Jack was safely off to work.

My hands were all of a tremble as I opened it.

"Dear 'Fun Loving Spirit', you could be the woman I'm searching for. Please meet me at *The Tudor Hotel,* 8 o'clock Tuesday next. I have made reservations to hopefully get to know you better. I shall be wearing a black leather jacket and a 'come-hither' smile!"

I don't remember ever spending much money on myself, but armed with a month's housekeeping cash I made my way to the *Live Girl Boutique* where only a week before I'd gazed longingly through the windows. Now I thumbed the coat hangers of skimpy minis and swayed my hips to the deep rich beat of the loud music. I revelled in a quick blow-dry and with a slinky black dress and lashings of *L'eau de Passion.* I was ready.

My patent heels clicked their way to the grand oak doors of *The Tudor Hotel.* I was early. At first I didn't see him.

Then he came from behind a pillar walking toward the bar.

"Oh No!" I mouthed silently. It was him – the milkman… the nervous middle-aged man who fumbled for change in his green *Meadow Milk* overall. He was now smoothing some stray hair over the shine of his bald patch, undoing the top buttons on a recently purchased black leather jacket. I felt sick, needed air but as I turned around to go I came face to face with Jack. He'd followed me. Eyes wild, he stared at the milkman, then back to me.

I felt like I was seeing Jack for the first time.

"Oh Jack, don't look at me like that. I mean it doesn't really matter. It's not what you think…" I teetered after him ridiculously on spindly heels. When we got back home there was his case in the hall way.

"Jack, what's all this about? We've got to talk."

"Don't say one more word," came his slow, guarded voice, "I followed you. Erma told me everything."

As if she had heard her name, the door opened and there she was, no longer the mousey widow – more like the *Merry Widow*! She gave Jack her own case and I felt chilled as she whispered with a grin:

"Keep it under your hat, it's just a bit of fun on the side!"

As Time Goes By

THE WINDS OF CHANGE

A gale was blowing up. As I looked out of the window I saw two cats chasing across the playground. If it were playtime it would have caused havoc, but now the yard was empty and they hissed and pounced in a world of their own. The wind encircled my mobile classroom. Its flimsy shell creaked and shuddered as I gripped the teacher's desk as if I were on the helm of a boat.

I decided to walk to the main school building. I felt safer surrounded by its long brick corridors. The wind could not disturb me here. Each footstep made hollow echoes as I passed empty classrooms, with chairs stacked on top of tables. Their leggy scaffolding, row after row obediently faced the blackboard still telling the order of the day. I had an hour to wait until my bus came. I didn't want to wait in the wind. I decided to kill time looking at some educational magazines in the staffroom.

Passing the Headmaster's locked office I heard voices. That was Ralph laughing. I smiled. Ralph was my Head of Department. Nothing seemed to bother him.

Flicking through a glossy supplement in the staffroom, I heard Ralph bringing somebody in.

"Hello gorgeous, still here? I'd like you to meet Clive. He's filling in for Mrs L until she's better. He'll be in the mobile next to you. Clive this is Jan."

"Hello Jan."

I suppose it began when he said my name. Nobody had ever said it that way. He had a deep soft lilt to his low Welsh voice. I stared unguardedly into his dark eyes.

"Would you show Clive to his classroom, Jan? I've got to pick up the kids."

"Well, if we can be quick before my bus."

"Clive will give you a lift," Ralph called as he walked away.

I was annoyed at his presumption, but Clive said it was no trouble. As we wandered down the corridor I found myself nervously chattering, explaining detail of school routines until I was tired of the sound of my own voice. I found it difficult to open the mobile classroom's door. As he pulled at the handle his hand brushed mine. I felt its warmth.

I showed schemes of work and textbooks to him. He nodded and murmured thanks. It was when he said,

"Where do you live Jan?". Our eyes met. He seemed to search the depths of my soul.

I did not answer but made a hasty apology and said I didn't want to bother him. I would catch the bus after all.

"See you tomorrow Jan."

He smiled like he knew me, and I rushed to the bus stop. The wind pulled and strained at my hair. The coat I was still fastening whipped at my legs. The gusts had lost their power to disturb me now. All I could hear was the gentle lilt of a low Welsh voice, saying, "See you tomorrow Jan."

The next evening after school he came into my classroom and sat on the edge of a desk. He began to chat.

"I've been in England for about a month. Before then I was in Africa for three years. My wife Mary wanted to be nearer to her mother, but I found it hard to leave."

"What was it like in Africa, Clive?"

"I liked to sit on the veranda of an evening and listen to the peaceful murmurs of the wildlife. It was hot and life was slow. No-one rushed. It's so different here."

"Is Mary happier now she's at home?"

"She says it's much better for our two girls to go to school in Britain. They can visit their grandmother. Mary likes a busy life. She's joined the WI and a local church group. We've only been here a short time, but she seems to be out nearly every night with different meetings."

"And you? Made many new friends?"

"Well there's you I hope?"

I allowed myself the luxury of looking into his eyes. We both knew that we wanted to be liked by one another.

Each evening after school Clive would sit and watch me put up displays or share my evening flask of milky coffee before I left to catch my bus.

After a couple of weeks Ralph asked if we could have a talk. During a lunch time he came into my room.

"It's a bit awkward really Jan."

"Why what's wrong?"

"Well you can tell me to mind my own business if you like. Did you know Clive is married? He's got two children."

"Yes," I replied, feeling embarrassed.

"Since he came back from Africa, he's unsettled. Sort of vulnerable… I don't think I'm putting this very well."

"Look, he comes in for a chat. He doesn't always want to go home straight away. There's nothing to worry about."

"Well I just don't want either of you getting hurt."

As he left the room tears came to my eyes.

I knew it wouldn't be long before evening chats were not enough. It came after Parents' Evening. We were at school late. Both exhausted. Clive came to my room looking tense and awkward. As if he had practised his speech, he said,

"Would you like to come for a drink with me?"

I paused. This was a turning point. I found myself saying:

"I'd like to. If Ralph and some of the others come too."

Clive looked as if I'd slapped him. He turned and walked out of my room. From that day on he avoided me. There were no more evening chats. I was hurt and disappointed. I wondered if I'd been foolish. I felt a great loss.

A few weeks later it was the School Fête. I was in my classroom fixing a ribbon around a box of groceries for the raffle. Two little girls came in carrying jars of jam and marmalade. I didn't recognise them. Then the eldest said:

"We're helping Daddy with his jumble stall and Mummy has sent us over with these for you." They were Clive's girls. They both had the same eyes and dark hair. Glancing over to his stall, a pleasant woman smiled at me and beckoned to her children.

As I carried the groceries out of the classroom the door was blown open by a sudden gush of wind. Pushing my way through, I grasped at the door to shut it. As I paused to look at the handle of the door I remembered the day we first met. The brushing of ours hands was the only time we had touched. Carrying the load to my stall, I struggled with the weight. I saw his wife nudge him to help me.

"You have two super girls Clive, and a lovely wife."

"Yes," he answered simply.

"Can we be friends again?" I asked sheepishly.

"We always were."

He left and went back to his family. The wind blew the stall's bunting in a melancholy dance. Ralph rushed to me with a bottle of wine for the table.

"Did you know *Camden Hill* wants a new Head of Department? It would suit you. Closer to home and it's a promotion. Phew! Doesn't this wind get you down?"

"I like it, blows away the cobwebs. Now about this job…"

THE PRIMROSE LINE

The train was due any moment and Lotsbury would be the first stop. Ever since I'd received the letter I knew I had to go back. Florrie had written to say Hollyoak was now for sale, after all these years.

I remembered my home at Lotsbury. I would walk again down a gravel path past Dad's allotment to the three railway cottages. Dad had been a signalman at the junction and very unofficially I had spent hours sitting on a little wooden footstool, red-faced with a cold back, huddled round a tall stove drinking sips of strong tea from a chipped enamel cup.

Dad would toast chunks of bread and tell tales of the *Townham Titch* and the *Byegate Belle*. The Titch would go on a shopping spree and the Belle for a trip to the sea. Then he would pause and listen to the tap, tap, tap of the signal box instruments and with a clean yellow duster he would squeeze and pull back the polished steel lever. The measured way he easily changed the heavy railway line points filled me with admiration for my dad.

The line in springtime was smothered in primroses. Dad said the gangers who worked on the line spent odd moments splitting the clumps and replanting to make it the prettiest line in England. They called it *The Primrose Line*.

For Lotsbury I knew it would be the Byegate Train – what a let down! Instead of the grandeur of steam from the Belle there came a diesel caterpillar, the front the same as the back! Surely this was not the Byegate train? Where was the guard? There was no station porter. Is this what was meant as an "unmanned" stop?

I sat near the front. I remembered "Smokey Joe", the old engine driver who would lift me high on to the footplate and I'd gaze at the hot red coals. The fireman would tell me how he fried a morning egg on the metal of his shovel. The cab was warm. All shiny blacks and polished brass.

I watched a beer can rolling around this coach floor.

As the train moved off, the soft "tiddleydum, tiddleydum" that I remembered was replaced by a slower mechanical "tee-dum tee-dum." I was so impatient to get there that the journey seemed to drag. I should have known there would be no primroses in January, just overgrown banks.

I gasped at a maze of *Monopoly* houses, rows of squashed buildings where fields used to be. Then I saw what was left of the Lotsbury signal box. It was black and derelict. The windows were broken. The wooden steps up to the door were rotted away and a large "KEEP OUT" sign was savagely nailed to the door. No red glow from the fire, no wave for the *Byegate Belle*.

I stood up ready for the station but the stupid little diesel went on! Why weren't we stopping? Helplessly I pushed my face against the grubby side window and there was

Lotsbury station – no hanging baskets, no chocolate and cream painted sign. Where were the *Great Western Railway* benches with the curly arm rests? No open welcoming door to the large oak waiting-room with plush red leather seats and the owl-shaped ticking clock. No staff, no ticket office – just a cold metal sign.

No trace of the gravel path – just parked cars and concrete and more and more houses. When I asked a passenger why the train hadn't stopped he said it had gone straight through to Byegate for years. I slumped back in my seat, tears of frustration in my eyes.

I came home by bus, didn't go to our old house. I came back to my daughter's house where I've lived for some time. My granddaughter Rosy met me.

"Where have you been Grandma? I've waited all day."

"I've been on a train ride Rosy, to a little village called Lotsbury. I travelled on the footplate of the *Byegate Belle* – a huge puffing steam engine. The fireman was frying an egg for his breakfast on a metal shovel. I chatted to a signalman who told me a tale of a little saddle tank engine called the *Townham Titch* who went out on shopping trips. On the way home I saw masses of primroses on the bank. The gangers split up the clumps and replant them, you know… to make it the prettiest line in England. That's why they call it *The Primrose Line*."

REMEMBER THE WELSH DOLL

It was a cold night when the blast of wind rattled the loose fitting windows of the draughty farm house.

"Thank God for a home on a night like this," Jack whispered to himself as he drew close to the fire. He looked deeply into the cracks of the red coals and thought of his mother. He imagined he could see her again rocking in her chair, but the vision disappeared and the only friend left was the constant ticking of the grandfather clock.

Suddenly there was a loud knocking at the door.

"Who is it?" he yelled through the door. No one had visited him for the whole year that he'd been alone, and it was late, very late.

"Uncle Jack! It's me, Lindy."

"I don't know you."

"Yes you do. I'm Clair's girl."

As if in a dream he unbolted the door and there she stood, wet and cold, a pale young woman in a grey stained coat carrying a battered old case.

"I've got your letter, the one you sent to Mum about Grandma being ill. She threw it in the bin, but I took it out and kept it. I remembered you'd been kind to me. You once bought for me a Welsh doll from Aberdovey."

A memory from over twenty years ago came back to him in a flash. He had visited Clair and this child only once. They had gone for a day to the sea. Little Lindy with soft curls and sunshine eyes had pointed to the Welsh doll in the shop window. He bought it on impulse. He could remember Lindy dancing in the waves. Her sandy fingers pulling open the bag, to once more peep at her new doll.

He opened the letter and read his words, "Let the past be forgotten Clair, she's your mother."

"What are you doing here?"

"I told her I was pregnant. I knew there would be a row but I thought when things calmed down… but no, she's done the same as her own mother did to her. I've nowhere to go. You're the only family I have."

Jack took her coat. It was soaked. He opened the door to his mother's room that he left untouched and showed her the drawers full of clean pressed clothes.

"Put these on. They may be big but at least they're dry."

Welling up, she hugged him but felt his embarrassment.

Warm and dry, sitting in her Grandma's chair, Lindy cradled the hot dark tea and, gazed at the fire with Jack.

Without looking up at her, he blurted out the words:

"What about the father?"

"He's a soldier," she said looking downwards, "I won't see him again. He's gone to Germany."

"Did he know?"

"Yes."

There was a long silence, then Jack said, "You can stay until we get you settled."

That night his mind was in a turmoil. He was alright on his own. Women always made him feel uncomfortable.

The next morning, just as when his mother was alive, he knocked her door. "Bowl of hot water for your wash in the sink. Back in an hour," then went about his work.

When he returned she was dressed and cooking his breakfast. The plain wooden table had the clean checked cloth that he never bothered with, and the second best crockery with a napkin to the side. He was about to protest when something in her quiet pride caused him to keep his comments to himself. He saw that she had put the Welsh doll on the mantelpiece, in pride of place. She was a little dusty with age but still bonny with eyes bright.

Lindy took over his mother's work as if she had always been there. The house was now spotless, the meals were tasty and on time. As they sat together in the evenings few words were spoken but there was a contented peace.

Jack went to the village once a week for supplies. One evening he said, unexpectedly:

"Lindy, I'm going shopping tomorrow, you come too. We'll need some things for when the child comes." It was the first time this was mentioned since she had arrived.

"But Uncle Jack, I have no money."

"Never mind girl, you've earned it. We'll leave at nine."

The village gossips knew things had changed at the farm as Jack's order now included such niceties as fruit for cakes, the odd bar of chocolate and a weekly order of a women's magazine. Now they saw the reason for the change. A pale young woman, noticeably pregnant buying enough wool for a baby's shawl and admiring, but not buying, a wooden cradle from the general store.

It was nearing Christmas and on cold nights Jack and Lindy felt happy as she knitted and he lovingly carved out a wooden cradle. Last year he hadn't bothered with Christmas. It was the first he had spent alone. But, this year Lindy put holly round the doors and even bought some cheap glass balls to hang on a sprig of fir. He had never known such contentment, until the letter came.

Jack thought it was for him. It was Clair's writing. He thought it was a card but inside was an *Airmail* letter from Germany. He knew he should give it to Lindy straight away but instead he put it in his pocket and went outside to his work, agitated. She noticed the change in him.

"Is there anything wrong Jack?"

She no longer called him Uncle.

"Lindy, tell me something, are you happy? Really happy?"

"You know I am," she readily replied.

"You don't regret coming here?"

"You're the kindest man I've ever met. Ever since you gave me the Welsh doll, I knew you were special."

It was then Jack slowly took the letter from his pocket and placed it on the table. She looked puzzled, but seeing her name and the *Airmail* postmark she opened it quickly.

"Oh Jack, he's home… he's home for Christmas. He wants to see me. He says he's sorry."

Jack said nothing. He just stared at Lindy, now she no longer looked like a woman, but more like the little girl with golden curls dancing in the waves.

She grabbed her things and packed hastily in the old battered suitcase she came with. He took her to the station and all the way she chatted incessantly of the soldier she had always known would come back.

When he arrived back at the farmhouse the evening was drawing in. As he lit the fire, there was a sudden chill in the air. All was so silent, just the ticking of the grandfather clock. He looked round at the holly and the fir with the glass balls, the half finished cradle, a magazine left open on her chair. Lastly his eyes rested on the Welsh doll, once treasured, but now left behind.

THE FLAG AT RANSCOMBE BAY

The news had spread so fast that all the town seemed to know about it before I did. *The Belvedere Hotel* was opening again. Some rich toff with more money than sense had fallen in love with its honey-coloured Victorian grandness, now all but faded with months of boarded windows. Life was about to change in Ranscombe Bay. Now folks would come and gaze out over its balustraded balconies across Little Head, Ronborough Hill all the way to Balacombe.

When I was a child I had walked past the large *Bentley*s parked outside. I remember seeing through the arched, heavy curtained windows the waiters in their black satin waistcoats serving ladies in straw floppy hats and dresses of layered pastel chiffon. As Mum sliced the bread for supper I had pronounced that, "One day I'd like to stay in *The Belvedere*." She had burst out laughing then looked at Dad. He kindly said, "Who knows what will happen."

Gradually there were no more *Bentley*s and the sign that welcomed guests had started to peel, worn by saltly winds and dusted with decay.

But now, the whole town bustled over the new opening and I needed a job. Several were advertised and at last in a tiny shared attic room, much smaller and plainer than the one I had at home – my wish had come true. I was at least, in a way, staying at the Belvedere!

There was a massive redecoration campaign, and although it was too early to see a tourist, we were madly getting ready. Dusty faded curtains with old gold tassels were dumped in the skip with the brass-handled doors soon to be replaced by modern fire safety doors. All the deep stone sinks and wooden ledges were replaced by flashy stainless steel surfaces where hundreds of piping hot tureens would be served. For several months we worked hard as a team, not actually meeting the new owner who lived in London. They said he would come when we were ready.

He arrived in March with his lady wife and a colleague, called Max who would become the new Entertainments Manager. All the maids, including me, stared at the black suited smooth cut of Max. His eyes were aware of every female in the room. And, if his eyes could speak they would have shouted, "I've looked at all there is, but you're the one I want," as he looked straight at me.

That night, from the formal black dress uniform we changed into our own clothes for dancing lessons with Max in the chandeliered Ballroom. He would teach us one by one to brush up our steps ready for the Tea Dances that would take place under the mirrorball. When it was my turn I could hardly dare to look up to his smooth, handsome face. He was hot and took off his jacket. My hand was on crisp white shirted shoulder feeling his warmth. His face, smoothly clean shaven came closer and I was engulfed by the heady fragrance of his spicy cologne.

He whispered, "How do you feel about the opening?"

Like a nervous child I stuttered, "Scared really…"

He held me closer, smiled and sang along with the song being played on the record player – "You may not be an angel. For angels are so few. But until the time that one comes along, I'll string along with you."

True to the words of the song he did. The next day, with a picnic cajoled out of cook with his smooth talk, we walked all the way to Ronborough Hill and sat on the seat next to the *Union Jack* flying well in the breeze. We stared out across the Bay. I giggled, chatted silly talk. He said little but put his arm around my waist. He remarked that his room was large and he could teach me some more steps. He lit candles, more romantic he said. We drank too much wine, the room took a warm red glow 'til I was sleepy and giving.

The harsh blare of the alarm clock at 5 AM jarred into my muzzy aching head. My roommate had said that Max had blatantly carried me back to the room at three in the morning. "Like used goods" was how she put it.

The next day he didn't meet my eye across the lounge area. I caught the message – the others mustn't know, to save our jobs. I waited for the furtive note that told me to meet him at our seat by the flag, or come once again to his room. But the note never came and as if the Manager knew, Max was sent on a last minute course on how to drive the hotel's new *Austin Princess*.

The opening came. A silver salver with BH grandly etched waited at reception with welcome *Mint Imperial*s for the arriving guests. We lined up in the ballroom for the official opening photograph, proud, pleased and exhausted.

They came as expected. The car park was full. Every cosy nook of the restaurant was filled with murmurings of between-course chatter. Dressed in glistening chandeliers the ballroom invited couples to dance. Max was accompanying any rich lady to swirl under the mirrored ball. What was he whispering in their ears? Did he sing the same song to each of them?

It was the talk of the maids how Max regularly lit candles and ordered wine for his room. Now there were rich takings which more than paid for the drives out to deserted places in the comfortable leather reclining seats of the frequently used *Austin Princess*.

I left quite suddenly. Something told me I had to get away. It seemed everywhere I went in the hotel I saw the Union Jack next to our seat through the window. Every corridor in the hotel seemed to exude a whiff of his cologne as if he had just walked by.

Mum wrote to me with a clipping from the local paper saying *The Belvedere* had been renamed *The Great Belvedere*. It was called the jewel in Ranscombe's crown.

About a year later, the telephone rang. Mum said, "Prepare yourself for a shock. *The Belvedere* – there's been a terrible fire." The whole place was ablaze. It could be seen all the way to Balacombe. It was a wreck. Two dead and about eighty rescued. "It seems that some stupid couple had candles lit in their room.", Mum lamented, "the flag is at half mast as the whole town mourns."

Carefully putting the receiver down I vowed to never return. "Oh Max!" I silently repeated over and over again.

Many years later when I was old enough to be a grandparent, I went on a mystery coach trip. As the vehicle slowly made its way down Beach Road I could barely steal myself to look up. Where *The Belvedere* used to stand was a tall red bricked municipal building with small utilitarian windows where busy clerks had no time to gaze wistfully out at sea views. Below was *The Belvedere Mall* – exclusive designer clothes and a coffee shop selling hand-made fudge. I decided to go in for a drink and there on the wall was a photograph of when *The Belvedere* was great. Underneath in a glass case was a tarnished silver salver with the etched BH still clear to see.

When I got home that night I opened my scrapbook to a photograph on a well-thumbed page. The staff are all lined up in the ballroom ready for the opening, and I can see him in the line smiling, the same smile. Once again I am the same young girl dancing under the mirrorball and his convincing, velvety voice sings *I'll String Along with You*.

For me, the flag is still at half mast at Ranscombe Bay.

Wishful Thinking

SANDY SHORES

It caught my eye like a fly by a web. I was captivated by the rustic glimmer of a faint white shell caressed by the boughs of a single apple tree. It was a caravan, quaint and small with a faded "For Sale" notice leaning against a murky cracked pane. It stood alone in the field. It seemed forlorn and forgotten, a memory of someone's yesterday.

I was on my way to a small fishing village in Cornwall but something about this lonely dwelling caused me to stop and look around. It was out of season, Easter time, but the spring sun played tricks with my thoughts and soon I was running the dunes barefoot all the way to *Sandy Shores*, our own caravan at Hayle.

It was no use looking back. This was thirty years later and I was the sole owner of the large and now lonely family house as my parents had both passed away. I was their only child. It was a strange feeling being completely alone. Could I call myself an orphan at my age? All I knew was the worry and the endless hospital visits were over. I was free but empty. I felt as adrift as a ribbon belt dropped from a dress. I now was alone without purpose. Yet something in this little caravan shone a beacon of hope in a storm. A promise of refuge. Perhaps a new *Sandy Shores*?

After the farmer had shown me inside he left me to sit and look at the van. It was warm and cosy, all I had hoped. There was a neat little scratched table between two faded beds. Within its walls were moulded large wooden encasements with dingy brass handles. Each window was shrouded with an ill-fitting grey net casting a shadow of a memory. I could keep it in this field as it was used for camping. I wanted it. I wanted that van so badly, I couldn't wait until the next weekend to start work on it.

The caravan consumed my thoughts and if I am truthful, my entire life. It filled the emptiness of the past weeks. I bought new, pretty material to cover the seats and make fresh curtains. I bought a small cooker, fridge and some bright new carpet. After I was finished the van seemed to come alive as its pretty orange curtains danced in the clean air from the open windows. When all was done, I proudly hung a small hand painted door-sign, "*Sandy Shores*."

It was beautiful and it was mine.

The next weekend was a bank holiday so I was not surprised to see a car pull into the field. Enjoying a leisurely cup of tea I watched them put up the tent. They were a young couple with two children who ran and giggled around the tent pegs. The man had his arm around his young wife's shoulders, admiring their newly erected tent. They smiled more than I'd seen people smile for a long time, looking lovingly into each other's eyes.

Each individual worked in harmony to set up their new territory and soon a barbecue was underway with wafts of freshly cooked food. They sat as children around a camp fire, teasing and laughing at each other's jokes.

The evening soon grew dark and they retreated back into the tent. A night light gave an orange glow encircling the happy family settling down to rest. I heard wishes of "good night" and imagined soft embraces. As the night grew ever colder I felt sure that they drew closer together for warmth and reassurance.

I couldn't sleep. I felt uneasy, unsatisfied, all seemed spoilt. The pretty curtains and warm-tufted carpet gave no comfort. I felt alone. Perhaps even more so than ever before. I stared at the shadows of the wooden encasements. Why had I not brought a photograph or an ornament or even a familiar picture? Everything in this van was new to me, and held no memories. I had thought it would be like *Sandy Shores*. But Mum had not leaned over this sink preparing vegetables for lunch. This was not the same scratched table where Dad and I had sat endlessly playing cards. This van had memories, perhaps happy or sad, but they weren't mine. This was not *Sandy Shores*.

I packed my clothes and left in the middle of the night to return to the large empty family home full of faded photographs, mementos and fond memories. I had driven swiftly down the country lanes and at the junction to a main road was a large litter bin. I stepped out of the car and hastily discarded the wooden sign which I had once excitedly cradled in my arms. On top of all the empty cans and ice cream wrappers from yesterday's picnics was the name of yesterday's dream – *Sandy Shores*.

THE RED DRESS

We'd had a row. Well – not a hot-headed yelling match. Michael wasn't like that. He slowly and very reasonably explained how it wouldn't be my sort of thing. Surely I could remember how office "do's" were full of office chat. I would only feel left out. But, I'd said if the other partners would be there, why couldn't I go? I never went anywhere. Then I remembered those leggy blondes from the typing pool. Last year I'd heard them gossiping in the Ladies:

"Well what d'you think of the Boss' wife?"

"Oh yes, Mrs Crump – more like Mrs Frump!" and then they exploded into giggles.

I supposed he was right and decided on an early night.

I hadn't long waved goodbye to Michael as he left for the party when the door bell rang. It was David, the university student who lived near my parents. He had brought around a case of mine. Mum and Dad were having a sort out of the roof. He happened to be there and offered to bring it to me.

I had only met him once before. I remember thinking how young and clean he looked – his hair still damp from the shower. He smelled soapy as he leaned near me to put down the case. He pulled at the lid. The lock was rusty and stiff but he managed to open it, and what a mess we found! Relics of my college days – doodled on cardboard files, empty picture frames, a cycling proficiency pennant – how did that get there? And at last a carrier bag. Inside, there it was – the red dress.

I pulled it out almost reverently, stroked the satin and closed my eyes as I hugged it to me. So much more than a dress – it was me, before Michael.

David stared at it, then to me, and I was lost for words. He started to say how beautiful it was and then impetuously said, "Why don't you try it on?"

I shook my head but then started to smile. I didn't need to be asked again. It fit like a glove – tight with its drop back and high slits to the thigh. I pulled the clips out of my hair and let it fall over my shoulders. His eyes told me that I looked as good as I felt.

"We need some dance music for a dress like that," he said, "Here's some old records in the bottom of the case." We knelt down and pulled out the old singles with tattered sleeves. There was my favourite – *Cliff Richard*'s *Do You Want to Dance*? I still had my old *Dansette* player from college and swiftly put it on.

Soon the room was filled with the rich fast beat and I was showing David how to dance *The Twist*. I said we could finish the bottle of sherry left over from Christmas. We giggled as we made a toast to "Good Health and Good Dancing!" We started to dance faster and faster, then slowly and more slowly and his arms slid around my waist to a soft romantic melody.

I cried when I told him about Michael – thoughts I had told no one else. It was the little things, like how I found the passenger seat belt had been pulled to a smaller size. How he'd lost his temper about the way I'd pressed his suit and how business trips away seemed more frequent.

David held my face in his hands, looked into my eyes and gently rubbed the tears away. I felt young but safe when he gently kissed my forehead. Then abruptly, he got up, wrote his phone number on a piece of paper and said:

"I'll come and collect you whenever you want," then he smiled and walked out. I was left alone.

Michael returned in the early hours. He found me gazing into the fire, hugging my knees, still wearing the dress.

"What is that?" he shouted, "So cheap and common!"

With as bold a voice as I could muster I asked,

"Are you seeing someone else?"

He stuttered, denied it vehemently, told me I had a fearful imagination. I waited for him to look at me. He didn't. He just turned away and went upstairs.

I stood up and all of a tremble walked over to the phone, the slip of paper in my hand. I dialled and mouthed the numbers defiantly, tapped my fingers impatiently. It rang and rang and then the receiver was picked up.

I whispered, "David?"

But a young woman's voice answered, "No we'd just got into bed – who's speaking?"

I said nothing and replaced the receiver.

Michael yelled down the stairs:

"Who are you phoning this time of night?"

"Oh nobody", I replied, defeated. It was a mistake.

I seemed to be making quite a few of those lately.

I undid the buttons and the red dress fell in folds around my ankles, hiding the crumpled phone number that had just dropped from my hand.

GOOD NIGHT GEORGE

It arrived in the post. She heard it drop on the well-worn mat, a brown thin envelope. She thought it was a bill and when she read it, she almost wished it had been.

Mill Parade was to be demolished. Reorganisation, re-habitation, modernisation – black print so neat and trite with such power as to change their lives. She had heard rumours, but the final words were proof.

She knew what George would say. There would be a scene. He'd go stamping to the county hall, furiously stuttering working-men's words. She could see it now, his flushed, purple face as sweat would streak his brow. She'd tried to tell him once how the other streets were going. He swore that the only way he'd leave *Mill Parade* was feet first!

She put the letter surreptitiously behind the King's plaque on the mantle. With half finished jobs and half finished cups of strong black tea, she bore the long hours until George would come home. She had decided not to tell him for the moment. It would give her time to think.

It was quarter to six. Best put the pot on the stove for when he comes home. She heard the familiar stamp of his boots outside the front door and, just as she had for many years, she opened it wide to welcome him home. He hugged her in the doorway with no mind as to what the neighbours would say. She took his tired canvas bag from him. He said, as he always did:

"Good to be home lass."

"It's good to have you home George."

She poured the hot water into the enamel bowl and he turned the brass tap to cool it. He rolled up his fraying sleeves and lathered his arms with smooth streaks of carbolic. She smiled while stirring the wholesome broth on the well-worn hob. He glanced at the newspaper while she served his meal. She saw how tired he was. He would soon finish after fifty years on the line.

Fifty years of timetabled, graft, grime and freezing cold nights on endless stations. How could they possibly live anywhere but here in *Mill Parade*?

Next door, they also had a brown envelope. They had once said that they might get to like it at *Ermine House*. There was no likelihood of that. She'd visited it once. There were pink carpets, pink walls and nylon rosy bed covers. All sat round in a circle on plastic arm chairs, dozing. She would not end her days in a stuffy pink room smelling of reheated dinners and disinfectant.

George, bless him he's having a snooze now.

She would wash up and then they would sit in front of the fire, his hand on hers as they listened to the radio.

How could she tell him about *Mill Parade*? How could it disappear? The street where they had played and squabbled together as children. She remembered their first shy kiss by the lamp outside her mother's door. This street was their first steps, first love, sad tales and kind memories.

Then she remembered. It had gone, a good five years since… and George had gone too.

She sighed, turned out the light in the plain pink room, pulled up the nylon rosy bed cover and whispered,

"Goodnight George."

HANDS AT THE WINDOW

I had to look. Would they be there again behind the dingy net? Like the rot in the frame, the hands were always there. An old woman's hands, entwined as if in prayer. I passed the damp terraces on my way to work. I never saw her face only the hands as she leaned against the window sill.

Today there were no hands. The house looked different. Too still, too empty. It disturbed me. Was she alright?

Perhaps she was ill? What if she died in the night? It was nothing to do with me. Why were my legs stopping, guiding me to lean over the iron railings and peer through the unwashed glass. All was black.

I'll knock at the door just to see if all is well. This is ridiculous. I don't even know her, but the iron knocker wobbled in my hand. A muffled voice came from behind the door and I found myself walking into a musty passage to the moaning from a side room. She was on the floor. With grey matted hair spreading over my shoulder I carried her to the sunken bed.

In the damp stale room, my eyes were drawn to the dust encircling the joins in a plastic mat. Near a worn-edged Bible a grimy medicine bottle stood in a sticky circle with a hair under its lid. She smiled as if remembering something.

"I was trying to reach my stick. I didn't leave it by the lamp. I fell off the bed trying to get it."

"Don't worry, you're all right now."

The shroud of neglect and stale filth choked me.

"I'll get you a cup of tea, won't be a minute. Kitchen through here?"

The table with a cracked plastic tablecloth held encrusted plates, a piece of dry bread and a half open tin of sardines.

"Do you have any tea?" I called.

"Tin on the ledge."

Yes, it did contain tea but only about two spoonfuls. Searching for the milk in the walk-in cupboard, I only found rings of rust and an isolated jar of mouldy marmalade. It was then that I remembered the flask and sandwiches I had packed for lunch. Wiping the dust from two cracked cups with a suspect towel, I got back to her.

"I have seen you," she said, "course I have, every morning. I don't go out now. Nobody comes, so I just wait."

Why did her smile make me ill at ease? It was as if she knew something that I didn't.

"Your cupboards are empty. Got any cash so I can buy you some food?"

With immediate trust she pulled out a small pile of five pound notes and gave me some. I left eager to help her.

By late afternoon you wouldn't have known the place. She was freshly bathed in a clean nightdress having had a hot meal. Her larder was scrubbed and well stocked. I looked around smiling, admiring my handiwork.

"Well, I'll have to go now."

"Wait my dear one last thing. I have something under the bed. I've kept it for when the time came."

I opened the dusty box and found two glasses on a silver tray and a bottle of sherry. The seal was broken, but it didn't look as if any had been used.

"You pour," she said.

I handed her a glass which she cradled in her lap. I took a sip of mine. It was warming. She watched me sip again. Her face began to sway. Were my eyes losing focus?

"We forgot to make a toast"

Her voice was distant. She raised the glass again to my lips.

"To my darling daughter. I knew you'd come back to me."

NEARLY HOME

I knew something was wrong the moment I opened the door. Photos from the ledge were missing; a mirror and a picture gone. Only my records toppled in the half filled unit. I ran upstairs and opened his side of the wardrobe. The solitary hanger playing a sinister seasaw told me all.

I had to admit the relationship had been dying for months, but as in any bereavement it was still a shock. In fact I panicked and caught the first available train to see my parents. They were stunned and grew old and vulnerable before my eyes. After an uncomfortable strained silence came a bubbling profusion of words: caring, suggesting, suffocating me. I went to bed. Mum came in, tucked the blanket under my chin just as she had when I was a child. It was then I knew that I shouldn't have come. I had to get back to face what was left behind. I packed and caught the midnight train to what I used to call home.

As the train pulled away from the platform I searched for an empty compartment. There were several. I don't suppose many would choose to travel at that time of night.

I had no ticket as a sign had said to collect one from the guard on the train. Alone now, I pulled the sliding door and took off my coat. Empty water bottles rolled and bumped into my heels prompting me to take off my shoes and put my weary feet on the opposite seat.

The gentle rock and tilt of the carriage was soothing and looking out of black night windows I could just see rows of street lamps guarding the curtained homes of families while they slept. It was just another night for them but it was one I would remember all of my life.

The train was to make two stops on my way home. It was after the first that my exhausted body was woken up by a young woman pulling at the door. She was very thin with a drab pale blue dress and dark rings under her eyes. She was carrying a baby and a wicker basket brimming with nappies and bottles of baby milk. I retrieved my shoes, sat up, smiled awkwardly and wished that she had found one of the other compartments.

"I hope you don't mind?"

"Not at all," I lied.

She had the saddest eyes I have ever seen. The baby, only weeks old and wrapped in a pure white lace shawl, was fast asleep. I was aware of the contrast between the baby's spotless clothes compared with her own. She stared at the baby's face then at me. She was nervous and kept rearranging the shawl and the basket, then pulling strands of greasy hair around her face.

For what seemed hours we both gazed at our own stark reflections in the black windows of the night. The baby stretched star fingers to his mother's face and began to cry.

"He's ready for his feed," she explained nervously. "I can't give him it as we are getting off at the next stop."

I was relieved to know that I would have the rest of the journey to myself. She looked up abruptly, and said,

"Will you do me a favour and look after him while I go to the toilet? There's not enough room for two of us."

I was surprised to be left holding the soft warm armful. With wide eyes he stared at me, attempting to focus. As she slid the door closed his small translucent face crumpled. The train started to slow down for the approaching station. I thought she would have to hurry up or she would miss her stop. But as I peered for the platform sign I saw a pale blue figure running to the station's exit, away from the train.

I stood up to shout no voice came. The child relaxed in my arms. I couldn't believe it. She had deserted him. What could I do? I had to find someone.

With baby in arms I searched each compartment. I found a man, eyes closed, mouth open, curled up with a bottle of whisky. A young couple sprawled in each other's arms, blissfully asleep. Where was the guard? The baby began to force a red faced cry screaming and demanding attention. I remembered the basket. Getting back into the apartment, I took the top off the milk and gave him the teat. Peace.

Perched on the edge of the seat I planned what I would do. When the train stopped I would find the guard, an official, or ring the police. They'd know what to do next.

Then I would go home.

But to what?

I began to visualise familiar rooms of our once treasured home now devoid of colour warmth or words. Just a shell, a cheap cardboard replica of what it once was. I remembered my father's words as I had got on the train.

"Put the past behind you, start to live again."

I watched the baby sucking at the feed. His soft lashes stroked folds of rounded cheek. A trusting little fist clutched tightly around my finger.

The train pulled up to my station. Heavily laden with baby and luggage I carefully stepped out onto the concrete platform. I walked with purpose in a sprightly step. The guard I had searched for came running from the train towards me. With a strong arresting voice he yelled:

"Hey Miss, wait just a minute."

I stopped and drew my breath with a prayer.

"Can I see your ticket?"

"Oh, I didn't see you on the train. I'll pay for it now."

"No matter." he said.

He looked at the baby. A smile came to his stern face.

"Contented little chap isn't he?"

"Yes he's just had his feed."

I tucked the shawl under his chin.

"He knows we're very nearly home."

YOUR DAY WILL COME

"I know it's hard," Mum said, "but your day will come."

The trouble is when you're sixteen, only just, and you've had to leave school to bring in another wage – it seems as unlikely as me walking past the chippy when I've still got money in my pocket.

Penford's wasn't my choice. Mum had seen the advert and here I was, the first day, brandishing a new grey overall, a foot too wide and a mile too long. I was pleased with my badge. A personal touch, having my name on it. All the world would know Miriam West now worked at *Penford's*, even if it was just as a sales assistant, a junior one at that!

The first hour perked me up. I learned how to operate the new electric till and was told never to open it except for a sale. I learned how to deal with a cheque – the paper money rich folks use. In a cosy training room with a row of quiet tills and empty chairs it was easy. But then, towering over me was a beehived woman with bright scarlet nails and horsey teeth.

Probably in the Fifties she could have been *Miss Blackpool* but at this moment she was the *Vivacity* representative from Perfumery. The problems began when she explained I had to "float" between the two perfume counters. The other was led by the *St Lorenz* representative. I soon learned that they were like vultures to their prey.

Each would pounce on a customer to grab their commission on their own brands. Well to keep the peace, when I found my first customer I sold a cheaper brand item so neither would be jealous. What a fuss! They flounced away furious! Each time a new customer came, I couldn't serve them as the ladies interfered, swooping down to sell their brand.

At one point beehive sent me to a glass cabinet to get a box of perfume for an embarrassed chap hovering at the counter. I saw the box was squashed so I asked if there was another to replace it. She found one under the till and begrudgingly wrapped it up. The young chap was delighted and thanked me for noticing, but she snarled and muttered that it was old stock to get rid of and he'd never have noticed if I had not said. They sent me for coffee and I breathed a sigh of relief.

The canteen was on the top floor and even using the new escalators it took an age to get up there. What a queue, and only a fifteen minute break. Apparently the new coffee machine was broken. One poor woman was pouring instant coffee, cup after cup in a long line. I decided to hop around the counter and give her a hand. When we got to the ones at the end I decided to give them a free doughnut as they had waited so long. The poor woman smiled and gave me a cup. I was just going to take a sip when the bossy woman from behind the till shouted that I had no right to serve food without wearing a white hat.

"You don't need to wear a hat to pour tea!" I called and some of the doughnut eaters began to cheer, but she pointed to the door.

By the time I got back half an hour had passed and beehive was tapping her watch.

"Please relieve Iris on Knitwear opposite. She's still waiting for coffee and it'll soon be lunch!"

I was now on my own. The Botany wool cardigans were laid out in rows according to shade, folded neatly like trussed chickens in a butchers. No one was buying so I thought I would change things to attract some attention. I took each cardigan and threw it in a mound, and it worked! It soon gathered quite a crowd. Before long customers were fighting over items.

There was one starchy woman with a pinched mouth who was just sifting through not buying. There was something odd about her. Perhaps she was a potential shoplifter?

Iris returned from her break and almost cried when she saw the state of her counter.

"But they're selling" I tried to explain. "I've sold two already". At that moment another customer held one out. I saw Iris charge the full two pounds, two and eleven pence but only ring up the two pounds and she left the small change on the front ledge of the till. She caught me watching her, then shut the drawer with money still on the ledge. I noticed the receipt was not given to the customer.

I thought she just had made a mistake so when she went to the stock cupboard I opened the till and picked up the change to put it in, but someone grabbed my arm. It was the weird woman with the pinched lips.

She was not going to get one penny. I pushed her with all my might and she fell back. There was a dreadful thud as her head hit the counter. She lay there in a monstrous heap, so still. I tried to shout, nothing came out. But there was a fire alarm on the wall. I took off my shoe and with the heel broke the glass. I pressed the button and very loud alarm bells rung all over the store. As if mesmerised everything came to a halt. Then there was panic.

Mothers grabbed children, one started to scream as hers had wandered away. Counters were left empty. People ran. Even on the escalators they shoved in front of others and headed for the doors. It was a strange feeling that all the confusion was because of me. I was still pressing the alarm, calling for help but no one was coming. Everyone ran away, leaving the motionless body at my feet.

The manager's face was stern as he pronounced:

"I think Miriam West will go down in history as the person who served for the shortest time at *Penford's*. It's not even tea time and I have a list of complaints against you".

The perfumery ladies had demanded I be removed from their department. Iris had claimed that I'd turned a neat display of quality knitwear into a jumble sale. I was banned from the Staff canteen for given away food. I'd opened a till without a sale, and set off a false fire alarm.

"You were even found red-handed with money in your hand, as you viciously attacked my store detective, who is recovering from concussion in the Medical Room! What have you to say for yourself?"

Well my mum often says that I'm never short of something to say, and somehow amongst the tears I spilled out my version of the day.

I didn't mean to get into trouble. I hadn't realised until he explained that Iris was fiddling the till. And as for the pinched face woman I didn't even know that stores had their own detectives. I didn't mean to hurt her.

"Now I wonder, if you were the Manager of *Penford's*, what would you say to a new employee who had caused so much trouble in a single morning?"

"I don't know what I'd say Sir, but if I had your job there's certainly a few changes that I would make."

He raised his eyebrows and stared at me.

After what seemed like an eternity of silence he said:

"What changes?"

I could hear my mum saying "Hark at our Miriam up on her soapbox," and true to form I didn't stop until I had finished describing all the ways I'd streamline the store.

He looked sternly at me, then pointed to the door.

"My office. Now. You're starting management training.

Getting to Know You

LITTLE BLUE NUMBER

Mum was late, late again. Sometimes I found a note. That day it read, "Defrost the bread. Put the rubbish out for the bin men and pop and get some chips for lunch." Weekends were no better. She worked all day Saturday, and Sunday was all washing, rushing and cleaning. I'd screamed at her last weekend, "It's just doesn't feel like home any more."

There was a pile of clean clothes to be put away.

Normally I left hers at the bottom of the bed. Such a big bed since Dad had died. She said *The Boutique* had been the making of her, but Dad would hardly recognise her now, with her jingle of earrings and click of spindly heels. Who did she think she was?

Her top drawer was left open so I decided to put her clothes away, and saw a letter on top of the dresser. It was my Danny's writing but Mum's name on the envelope. I wondered if I shouldn't read it, but what would my boyfriend possibly need to write to my mother about?

"Dear Lynne," it read.

Since when did he call Mum by her Christian name?

"Thanks for our chat. I don't know what I'd have done otherwise. It meant so much to me. I've decided that you're right. Thank you, Danny."

"PS Here's your earring, found it in the front of my car."

My head began to spin. I sat stunned, perched on the edge of the bed staring wide eyed at the dressing table mirror. I remembered her teasing voice:

"You sit there dumbstruck when he comes into the room. He's too old for you. A boy of eighteen wants to play the field. You should concentrate on your exams and help me more around the house."

She'd said that, when all the time she was meeting with him in secret! I threw the letter back on the dresser. I felt like tearing her new lacy underwear and smashing the mirror with her expensive perfume.

Secrets. We never had secrets. Until now, she'd always been there. I remember her clean starched apron and rosy cheeked face. The house used to smell of warm cakes and now it was cold and empty.

Mum had sold the two up two down cottage in Melville and with Dad's insurance money she bought the bungalow at the Crescent. She said she never saw anyone when I was at school. It was just a life of gazing at row upon row of clipped lawns, white fences and a hundred identical lean-to garages. She had tried the coffee mornings but couldn't stand the bickering behind people's backs.

She had called *The Boutique* "a new beginning." People said she looked brighter, younger and when she was offered the promotion to manager I seemed to lose all that was left of Mum as well as Dad. Our home could have been Euston station. We came and went, lived side by side, parallel lives, we hardly spoke.

Danny had been my only crush. He was different. Dark eyes and the looks of a film star. In comparison, the other local lads were like buffoons. Our families were close neighbours and friends but after Dad had died we didn't see much of them.

"It's hard," Mum had said, "they don't know what to say."

A week before, Danny told me he was going to try to join the army. His parents were against the idea and he told me he'd apply anyway without them knowing.

I had to talk to him so I picked up the receiver and dialled his number. His mother answered.

"It's me. Can I speak to Danny please?" I didn't have the faintest idea what I was going to say.

"I'm sorry dear," she said "he's not here."

"When will he be home?"

She was silent, then in a trembling voice said, "He just packed his bags and went. I don't know where he is or what's wrong. I don't know why he's doing this."

With a weak, "Sorry," I put the phone down. It had to be because of Mum. He'd fallen for her and couldn't tell them. He was no better than Mum. She didn't have the guts to tell me either.

I opened the wardrobe door searching for evidence. There was one of Dad's jackets, the old dog-tooth check. I had a photo of him wearing it at Bradmore Bay. He'd laughed, frantically making adjustments to the camera for me to take it. The jacket still smelled of him. "Oh Dad," I cried and buried my face into the sleeve.

Right next to it was a new dress, too short, too tight and much too young for her. I yanked it from the hanger and crumpled it into a ball then raced down the stairs and grabbed the kitchen scissors. Kneeling on the floor with shreds of blue all around me I cried for all I had lost: Dad, Mum and now Danny.

I heard the rattle of the dustmen's lorry, grabbed all the pieces of blue and ran to the bin. I stuffed the evidence into a black bag and carried it out to the men. One winked as he took it from me. Could he tell that I'd been crying?

I watched the hall clock. She should be home by now.

The phone rang. It was Danny's mother.

"Hello love, is your Mum there?"

"No, not yet."

"I'm glad to tell you Danny's home. We are so grateful to your Mum". I stood listening, dumbfounded.

When Danny tried to join the army, he had needed to show his birth Certificate. His mother told me sheepishly that this was how he'd discovered that he was adopted.

"We meant to tell him, but never seemed to find the right moment. Must have been such a shock. Was in a real state when he bumped into your Mum in town."

Danny had told Mum everything. She'd taken him under her wing, to a cafe, bought him coffee, not let him leave 'til his mind was in a better place. She told him that even with all the mistakes that she had made, she never stopped loving me, and his adopted parents were just the same.

I'd just put the receiver down when the door opened and there was Mum.

"Sorry I'm late love, went to the jewellers because one of my earrings, the clip had come loose."

"Mum, I've something to tell you."

"Hang on, I've got something important to say. I've sent my resignation in to head office. I was thinking of what you said about this not feeling like home. I was so busy distracting myself from missing your Dad, that I was ignoring the person that I love most."

We hugged each other then she took off her coat and said,

"You know, I've been talking to your Danny. He's had his problems but I've changed my mind about that boy. You should invite him for tea sometime."

I was about to say that I'd like that, when she added:

"Oh! I forgot, I got you a little surprise in the sale on my break yesterday. You should wear it for Danny – a beautiful little blue number."

AUTUMN LEAVES

She arrived loudly screaming in the height of October.

The leaves were rapidly changing, and so would my life. She had arrived when those trees were golden, umbrellaed by a wash of corn-flower blue. This was always my favourite season, so we called her Autumn.

She had a blaze of red hair and brown eyes, just like her Dad. Both had freckled smiles and kind words. Through the cold days of little money she warmed us with her first words and friendly ways. I couldn't believe we could deserve such a beautiful child.

The school bell rang and she ran ahead, not holding my hand now, forgetting to wave as she ran through the gate. I was no longer part of her world. I didn't even know what she had for her lunch! She would return chatting adoration for Miss. All I said was wrong. Miss always knew best. Miss was in the realms of a heavenly dynasty and I, a mere mortal who washed clothes and filled plates.

My lovely Autumn no longer sat on my knee but ran to the door for Daddy. He knew what she thought. He knew her days as I stood by the sink.

When did skipping rope days turn into dark truculent secretive times? Giggles were kept for classmates and sullenness for me. After several nights, late arrival home turned into no arrival home. Our home, she said, was no longer where she wanted to be.

"He loves me!" she had screamed down the phone but all that loving turned into a heap of "if only"s and she was left alone with a child soon to be born.

I phoned and cried. I wrote and cried. I cried again and again and when at last no tears would come, I waited.

It was when the first leaves began to fall she came back. Her eyes were deadened by exhaustion. She slept restlessly in her bed surrounded by posters and childhood mobiles.

These days, next to her bed is a cot. Once more, my little girl has her freckled smile and kind words, just like her Dad, but now, she also shares her days with me.

THOMAS

Thomas was now a Godly man.

The new curate had asked Thomas if he would be a lay reader and take the six thirty Evensong. He had been a sidesman for years but this was different. So different to the six days a week he cycled to *Harvey's Printing Press* where he type-set, type-casted and totally unnoticed.

But, this was Sunday. He briskly straightened his starched white surplice. He was proud of his reflection in the vestry mirror. Best shoes, worn but polished, army-style stood to attention. He smiled, thoughtful of his duty and with an about turn, marched stiffly to light the altar candles.

Six old ladies were the congregation. They used to dribble in unnoticed, but now Thomas would hover over as the heavy wooden door creaked shut, swoop down, and with an oyster-like grip, shake their hands, drowning them with oozing benevolence until they escaped to disappear into the darkest pew.

One of the six was a short mouse-like creature who gazed at Thomas in the pulpit, with adoration dancing in the dew of her eyes. As he read his proclamation of doom and disaster, fear and retribution, hell and damnation, fire and brimstone – a fat lady fidgeted and looked at her watch.

Oblivious, he raised his fist to deliver the last merciless message, then theatrically bowed his head. He paused dramatically. A great feat performed. Some dozed, others straightened and coughed while the mouse silently applauded with wonder in her eyes.

The candles were reluctantly put out. The heavy door locked. Thomas walked home, almost sprightly until he felt the cold metal cycle clips in his overcoat pocket. His pace slackened as he thought of *Harvey's Printing Press*.

Brushing his shoes on the bristled "Welcome" mat he noticed them, creased with dust and showing their age. They also would have to wait six long days until once more worn by the Godly man.

THE JOLLY MAN

I heard the factory siren and knew it was the end of his shift. Soon Billy would be walking down Mill Street with the happy swagger of his dusty boots and grimy hands.

I waited for him, as I had every day of that summer holiday. It started after I had fallen off my bike and he found me, feet in the gutter, bike heavy on my legs and crying. I didn't hear his footsteps but when he bent down, I looked up at a familiar friendly face. Billy had come to our house once or twice before. He was a friend of my Dad. We all liked him.

"Now what's up then, you alright?" he smiled and took out an old first-aid tin. I was going to say I didn't need anything, when I saw the remains of his lunch. He pulled out a piece of fruit cake.

"You hungry?"

The cherries were tempting so I nodded, brushing a stray tear away from my cheek.

After that day he always kept me something, half a sandwich, a biscuit, just a treat to look forward to. Sometimes he would put his hat on my head and squat down, waddling on his heels, pretending to be a baby by my side. I laughed until my sides hurt. Some days he would lift me up until I could almost reach the light in the lamppost outside our house. He would tell me I was the prettiest girl in Mill Street. I knew I wasn't but I was glad that he'd said so.

Mum teased me and said it was the titbits that I was after. All I knew was that he was a jolly man and meeting him on his walk down Mill Street from the foundry to his digs was the best part of my day.

As soon as he had moved in with Mrs Lavender the whole street had taken to him. I heard my mum in the corner shop, saying to her friend:

"Such a pleasant young chap. Not frightened of hard work and a lovely manner."

I started walking up to the factory each day hoping to meet Billy as he finished his shift. He was at the entrance leaning on the railings chatting to a workmate when I arrived.

"Hello poppet, how's life with you then?"

"Alright thanks Billy, shall I carry your tin?"

"There's nothing in there today," he teased and began the usual game of passing it from one hand to the other behind his back. I grabbed the tin from his hand and retrieved a Garibaldi. Eagerly I began to munch. I took hold of his hand and stretched large steps to match his own as we walked home together.

Our neighbour's son also worked at the factory, and it was over the garden fence that I first heard the news.

"I hear young Billy's taken up with the Cartwright girl from the office. He'll have his work cut out with that one. Right jumped up sort she is. Her mother ruined her."

I didn't see him for about a week. I waited by the gate but he didn't come. One of his mates had smirked when he said Billy had changed his shifts. He said it was to fit in with his courting.

It was a Thursday night and I was coming home from my weekly piano lesson, which I hated. I had bought four pennyworth of chips as compensation. I was trying to finish them before I got home then I wouldn't have to share them with my nuisance of a brother. As I turned into Mill Street I saw him leave his digs.

"Hey Billy, you look posh."

With smart drainpipe suit and hair slicked down he looked like a film star and smelled like a chemist shop.

"Yes I'm out on a date poppet."

"Someone special Billy?"

"Oh very special. She means the world to me."

He waved a rushed farewell and left me feeling alone and rather ridiculous with music bag in one hand and the remains of cold chips in the other.

The autumn term started and the long evenings came. I had not seen Billy for weeks.

I heard that he had married Amy Cartwright and they were living in a flat in town. I missed his laugh and silly jokes.

One day Mum wanted some vinegar to make mint sauce for Sunday lunch. I ran down the hill with a pop bottle to the off-sales of *The George Inn*. Waiting my turn I could see through to inside and it was then that I saw him. He was red faced, elbows on the bar, his tired eyes searching for an answer in the bottom of a whisky glass.

It was almost afternoon closing time so I ran around the front of *The George* to meet him. I was shocked. He could hardly walk straight. He was haggard and old.

"Billy, it's me!"

"Me who?" he shouted, "Oh it's you. What do you want?"

"What's wrong Billy, can't you walk?"

"It's nothing to do with you, go away kid, go home."

I wanted to help him but he shouted at me and I cried as I ran home to tell my mum.

Some weeks later I heard that he was back in his old digs. His wife had left him for somebody else. I asked one of his mates about the times of his shifts and decided to meet him. He was not the same. A slow step with hunched shoulders and such weariness in his eyes.

"Hi Billy."

"Oh hello poppet, why are you here?"

"Just come to meet you."

"What for?"

I looked up with a twinkle in my eye. "Well Mum and Dad said you could come round for a meal if you want to some time. My mum makes the best cakes."

I held out a clump of fruit cake. "I saved you a piece from my tea, its got cherries."

"I'm not hungry."

"Course you are. Everyone needs to eat."

I grabbed his hat, squatted down and began the baby walk hiding the cake behind my back. A faint glimmer, then a real smile set his face alight. He chased me for the cake. We tripped, fell over and laughed. I hugged him, so glad to have my jolly man back.

FOLLOW MY LEADER

I knew at the beginning. He was just too willing. As soon as his car arrived at the restaurant he seemed to fall over himself to open her door. He even undid her seatbelt as if she were a child. When we were called for the meal it was embarrassing to see how he arched over her, oiling and oozing while she kept rearranging her knife and fork.

It had always been the firm's custom to wine and dine the new staff. She was the new junior secretary, all lip-gloss and nerves. She avoided all the eyes. He sidled his chair closer to share the menu. She leant away, trying not to look uncomfortable. He rested his elbow on the back of her chair. She shuffled to perch on the edge and gripped the table so hard that her knuckles became white.

He put his arm all the way round her seat and she abruptly stood up knocking the cutlery to the floor. She started stuttering that she did not feel well. He coiled his arm around her shoulders, his breath too close. Then she pushed him away and ran to the door.

I ran after her out into the car park, and showed her to my car. She was relieved. I don't know why I drove her back to my house. I suppose it was because it was close. I didn't know where she lived. I didn't even know her first name. She looked so young, perhaps not much older than my eldest daughter. All I wanted was for her to feel safe. Looking a little embarrassed, she smiled for the first time.

I sifted through unwashed mugs and swilled two under the cold tap. She was my only visitor since my David had left. I looked around at the mess in the kitchen but she just smiled as she wrapped her hands around the warm mug for comfort.

The first words she said were, "Thank you," softly, and then she told me her name was Laura. She said that Clive had been just a pest at first but now he had taken to following her at lunchtime, even waiting outside her flat to offer a lift to work. She had seen his white car parked across the road late at night. Tears filled her eyes.

She was sitting in the same chair as David had when he said he was leaving. There had been tears in my eyes too.

The cat was scratching at the back door. I let him in. It was strange to think that when the kids were small the cat was for them. I had hardly noticed him but now he was the other mouth to feed, the only welcome at the door. He squirmed in and out of my ankles purring for food. I reached into the fridge for the opened tin of cat food and scraped some into his unwashed dish.

I explained to Laura about the firm. It was a long established solicitors and Old Man Peters ran it the way he always had. I hadn't dared tell him about Kate leaving over four months ago, again because of Clive. It would just cause another row, and nothing would change.

I said that I was going to have a talk with Clive, firmly warning him off bothering Laura any more. If he didn't behave I'd have to finally say something.

"The trouble is," she said, I'm scared to go home. He's sure to be waiting for me outside the flat."

The cat had now curled contentedly on her lap and she was stroking him gently. It was getting late so I said she could stay the night if she wanted. I had been sleeping in the spare room. The double felt so empty without David. She could use the main bedroom. When I made the suggestion she seemed relieved. I started to show her around the house.

The dining room was tidy, all but the dust. Lead crystal glinted from the cabinet with the bone china tureens we had used for entertaining. I showed her into the main bedroom. David's aftershave was still on the ledge. Laura stood by the door and said, "Goodnight" and I put my alarm on for the next day.

I woke to a rattling in the kitchen. At first I thought it was David and then I remembered. The air smelled sweeter than recent times. Perhaps she'd used the air freshener.

The kitchen was a transformation. There were no dirty dishes, table clear all but a knife and fork and she was stirring beans on the stove.

"Couldn't find any eggs," she said, "will beans on toast do?" I sat down to a proper breakfast for once.

Old Man Peters didn't approve of the office women "gossiping" outside of work. I dropped Laura off nearby and went to park in my usual corner. The parking spot was already taken by Clive's white car. I vowed to have it out with him, but the moment I entered the building I was instructed to go straight to Peter's office.

"Well it's like this," he said, "There's word around the firm that you and Laura were out on the town last night."

I braced myself for a lecture on workplace etiquette.

"Now don't you worry," he continued, "I've known David long enough to know he wouldn't have any of that nonsense. It's about time you both came around for dinner again. How about tomorrow night?"

There was a knock at the door and in walked Clive.

"Ah now," the boss pronounced proudly, "here's the man of the moment. How've you been getting on?"

The old man beamed with pride. "He's my daughter's boy you know. Clued up is my grandson. I've told him if he follows my lead, he'll do all right for himself."

A Time and Place

GLOUCESTER'S CHILD

I went to an old Victorian primary school in Widden Street. It was surrounded by spear-like railings and it had arched sash windows. We chanted times tables, sat in rows of flip-top desks ironed to the ground. The teacher sat in a lectern desk and cast an eye on us struggling in silence to find "how many men could dig that hole in how many hours?" The treat of the week for me was to enter the holiest place, the staffroom, to wash the teachers' cups.

We would use the pure soapy liquid my mum could not afford, and I remember the clean, fresh pine fragrance from the bubbles. I felt like a lady with perfume all the way home. On Fridays we would go to the rich school, well I thought they must be rich as they had what seemed like miles of grass and trees. We sang all the way in a green double-decker bus. We were going to play shinty with the privileged children of Tuffley. The air felt good and there was space. It reminded me of holidays when we could cycle to Painswick Beacon for bread and jam picnics.

On Saturday mornings we would queue in the drizzle for *The Ritz* picture show. We cheered for *Flash Gordon* and booed the oppressors as we fidgeted in sixpenny red velvet tip-up seats. We swung our legs as we munched popcorn. After the show I would shop at the *Co-op* in Barton Street. I would carry the milk and bread tokens in a tobacco tin and had to give Mum's number so that she could claim her dividend. As the loaf was wrapped in soft white tissue I noticed how crisp the crust was, and I would peel and nibble before I got home.

On the occasion of new shoes or coats we would go to town. The *Bonmarché* stood in King's Square. In later years I worked there wearing a neat black uniform and red badge. During my lunch hour I sat in the roof garden knowing that all the busy shoppers in the car park and bus station below were unaware of me. My favourite department was toys. One Christmas I worked in the toy fayre and we drank sherry secretly in a doll's tea-set behind the counter.

Carnival time in Gloucester was the highlight of the year. We queued to watch garish floats and each day of the fortnight we walked to the Park to stare at the lights and bustle of the fair. The last night firework display was a real family treat and we oohed and aahed in between mouthfuls of hot-dogs and onions.

The years have seen many changes. Gloucester was and is now a busy centre. It has changed beyond recognition in parts but when I am travelling back from long journeys, I am always glad to see the orange glow of street lights where the cathedral tower stands proud and welcomes home Gloucester's child.

ONE AUGUST MORNING

On a dusty pavement, burning and dry, we licked too slow the ice-creams that dripped down our grimy elbows. It was too hot to run.

We swung jam jars tied with string – threw them past the weeds of the River Twyver, caught sticklebacks, silver and sad, watched their eyes… then set them free.

Sitting on a metal bath covered in a moth-eaten blanket, we sipped *Tizer* and ate grapes – let the juice run in red raindrops from our chins.

We watched ants run in confusion in a dry puddle hole where we had launched lolly-stick boats. Scurrying and turning – didn't they know this was a slow time? A time for sitting with knees under your chin, poking your toes through holes in your sandals, listening to far away arguing voices as they did the once a week turn of the mattress.

I could hear the clank of an errand boy's pedals – fast, late for his delivery. A child is squealing as he topples from his pram-wheel trolley. There's the regular slap-jump, slap-jump of the frizzle-haired girl next door, practising her skipping – *Clark*'s red sandals on a blue slate yard.

Mrs B's pegging out, struggling with a cotton twill sheet, still *Omo* damp with mangle creases. I can smell the sweet wafts of cinnamon, nutmeg – Mum's baking for Dad's bag. Too early to have washed the bowl yet. She'll say, "Wash your hands first," and I'll whine, "Oh Mum," and when she'll turn away I'll flick a forbidden finger full of dripping cake mix from the earthenware bowl. I'll wash under the brass tap that runs too fierce, splashing the wooden drainer, pounding the stone sink, splattering away the pavement dust and washing away all the sleepiness from my sticky morning face... did water ever taste so sweet?

It's a million years since I've washed my face in that old stone sink, yet when memory is kind and time is slow and giving, I can close my eyes and through the mists discover once more the safety and contentment of just such a warm, welcoming August morning.

TALBOT WAY

It's black and cold at Talbot Way. Silence blows round a tottering fir trees – leggy, too scant to cover the white tip-up garage doors, same as the other hundred in another thousand rows. One single lamp paints the golden empty road and tries to keep awake folk who are tired of the day.

All have put out clean clinky bottles, still frothy damp from the dregs. Muffled light peeps from upstairs curtained worlds, each sleeping within a hand's touch of each other, yet some have never spoken.

The young marrieds giggle in a king-sized bed. Their eyes as close as their bodies' heat. They cannot hear the silver drops of pain on a tear-sodden pillow, only a step away, or the slam of a door and the wretched clench of a fist that surely has the power to blitz the thin glass of one man's tender shell.

A TIME AND PLACE

The headphoned boy still lulls to his overture, the arc of paradise dancing between his own ears. The blackness has stripped the woman who wore the correct finery to meet the day and left her with stark tossing thought, twisting and biting at hope.

Now the lights have gone from the houses and the orange lamp waits its turn until dawn. The rows of same shaped windows and same size bricks surround the beds of those that sleep smiling or those that fret the hours. Each a private pigeon-hole to spend a life, yet, when the light comes and curtains are drawn to a new filled milk bottle morning – each will gather strength to leave the safety of their front door, to face the whirling gush of all that blows outside, far from the tottering fir trees of Talbot Way.

Tales of the Unexplained

THE SIX O'CLOCK BUS

If it had not been pelting with rain in the blackest winter night I could remember, I would not have sheltered in the old bus stop. Rain shot to the ground as if to prove its power. I could only think of my hot warming meal waiting back at Mrs Bradbury's but it was senseless to go on. Perhaps it would ease for a while.

What a God forsaken place! A gloomy industrial town miles from all that I knew, but it would not be long 'til my course was be finished and I could get back home. Watching the rain I became aware that I was not alone. I heard someone softly humming. Standing in the shadows stood a beautiful young woman. Although dressed in drab grey clothes, her face was radiant and her eyes bright.

"Oh I didn't see you there. What a dreadful night."

She smiled and said, "It's a lovely night."

"You must be joking!" I shrugged.

"Well it is for me. I'm meeting Eddy on the six o'clock."

"Eddy… Eddy Ashcroft. He's my young man. Tonight he's going to ask my Dad if we can be wed."

"And what will your Dad say?"

"I'm not sure, but probably he'll say, Bett, you're still young, money's short and where d'you think you'll live? Not in Nelson Parade with the six of us!"

"And what will you say?"

"Well, I just know that when he meets him he'll know he's right for me. He's just finished his apprenticeship at *Kirby's*. He'll be working on the presses and that's good pay if he's not laid off."

"Any chance of that?"

"No there can't be, there mustn't be. See, me and Eddy… no one is like me and Eddy."

She smiled, a smile the warmth of which I had not seen for many years. I could not help but envy her. She barely noticed me as I left. She was in a world of her own and I was late for my meal.

"Well I'd better be off then. Good luck for tonight."

She didn't answer, just kept searching for the bus with hope and excitement dancing in her eyes.

The rain fell torrents without catching its breath. Pushing open my landlady's door I was met by wafts of Irish stew.

"Hello Love," she beamed from the steamy kitchen. "Dinner's ready but it can wait. You go and change before you catch cold."

Warm and dry, I started my meal and she put down the local newspaper.

"I don't know why I buy it. All the news is bad and they say more rain tomorrow."

"Does it mention men being put off at *Kirby's*?"

"*Kirby's* you say? Good Lord no!"

The doorbell rang.

"Ah that'll be the old boy who lives on his own. We're going down the Social. It's nice he gets out now. For years he just stayed home."

A grey haired man shyly took off his trilby and smiled nervously. Mrs Bradbury took his arm.

"Let's introduce you. This is my old friend Mr Ashcroft."

"Any relation to Eddy Ashcroft?"

He was puzzled.

"The one that works at *Kirby's*?"

"What d'you mean?" his voice began to falter.

"The one who hopes to marry Bett?"

At this he began to stagger, gripped the hat stand and it toppled down. Mrs Bradbury tried to help him.

"Edd for goodness sake sit down here."

"How did you know?" Edd stuttered.

I then told him about my meeting with Bett waiting for the six o'clock bus. His eyes were as if in a trance. He tried to speak but no words came. Mrs Bradbury knelt before him.

"It's all right Edd. It must be a mistake."

She turned to me and whispered:

"*Kirby's* was pulled down years ago and Bett died in a direct hit on the bus shelter in the war."

The rain thrashed at the window pane, as if trying to get our attention. We sat speechless, watching Edd. Slowly, so slowly the worried lines seem to slide from his face and for the first time in hours, the rain eased. First to a gentle whisper, then a beautiful silence.

In the stillness I could hear Bett humming, and see her eyes light as at last she saw the six o'clock bus arrive.

A SONG FOR TILLY

"Oh Tilly, please don't go, I'm sorry. I'm sorry."

"There, there Mr Heim. Don't you worry. It's alright."

That voice again – the calm firm one. I could hear the words, not see their faces. These mists, they swirl back and forth, just like the sea mists. Yet it was all so clear when I first saw her, and that moment would change everything.

"Fancy inheriting a caravan dumped in the middle of God knows where! No doubt the money will come in for school fees, or perhaps Crete again this year? But a caravan? I ask you. They said old Albert was odd…"

"*Different* was the word my Dad used. I never went to visit my uncle. I think I'll go and see the van."

There it was – I'd said it. No planning, no thought. It just felt right. Truthfully, I must have been waiting for an excuse to escape.

At Kele Bay the mists hugged low and wrapped like a scarf around the pathetic lime green caravan. It was so old and neglected, sheltering from the winds of time under the kind boughs of a willow tree.

I smelled damp the moment I opened the door. There were old blankets, walls stained from long unused gas lamps. A black kettle stood waiting on a cold hob. I was ready to lock the door and leave, but then a ribbon of sand caught my eye. It lead through the gorse and up over the cliff. As I reached the top, there was a wide open view of Kele Bay. The sunlight painted a silver blanket on waves which foamed and licked the small rocky cove.

I lay on top of the hill and closed my eyes listening to the hypnotic lapping of the tide. The wind was blowing gently on my face. It was then I felt a presence. I opened my eyes and she was in front of me, staring. She had white blonde hair and the edges of her dress fluttered in the breeze. She wore no shoes. She was so beautiful, a young slender woman who left me speechless. I was so in awe of her dark blue eyes now smiling at me.

"I saw you in the caravan," she said simply.

"Yes," I was the one now staring. "It's a rum old place – needs too much work."

"I love that caravan", she said, "I often come here to this hill. I like dancing. I dance and this is my stage. With the waves and the breeze, I belong here. I feel it's mine."

"Dance for me," I whispered, and as if the sun were her spotlight, the sky a shimmering drape, she began gentle pointed steps and turns. She etched swirls and curves with her body. I was entranced with her loveliness. All the time she was humming a familiar tune. What was it called?

I wondered if I had really been alive until then. Seeing her mingle with the clouds, the ground, the air – it stripped me of all pretence. With eyes wide open I was fragile to her power, yet knew I would forfeit my life at that moment, just to be with her always.

We walked hand in hand back to the dusty old caravan. We sat cross-legged sipping black tea from metal mugs. She cradled the warm drink in her hands and said,

"You're so like him. So like Albert."

"You knew my uncle?"

"Yes. Years gone, when he was younger. He saw me dancing and he said he would capture me in oils."

"Did he do it?"

"He tried but I wish he hadn't. At first we would talk, easy talk – then he'd say 'Dance, Tilly love', then he would sketch. He began again and again. He could never get it right. He would get cross. He'd shout. Once, he cried. He'd say 'it's the wrong time, it must be the wrong time'. One day he was so ill and tired that he said he'd burn all his paintings, but I hid the unfinished sketches in the outhouse – he never knew. I'll show them to you."

And there she was on the paper, Tilly dancing to her song.

"It's so sad he never finished them." I said. "I've always wanted to paint. Took an evening class once. Teacher said I had some skill. Somehow there's never been time."

She sat up, her eyes on fire.

"Paint me," she said. "I know where he kept his paints, some never even used. Please do it for me."

She came to me. Hands on my shoulders, her lips on my cheek. The closeness was too much, her body too near. I lost all thought of all I should or would want to know.

We loved in a frenzy, innocence lost, she lay warm in my arms, sweet smile on her lips. This was it. This was the painting. She lay there, timeless as I outlined her shoulders, love blending with each brush stroke. When at last she saw it, she was overjoyed. She laughed delightfully and dissolved into my arms. In the haven of that place we lay and slept entangled so close as if we were one for always.

"Can you hear me Mr Heim?"

It was that firm voice again.

"It's always the same. People say they can hear you and to keep on talking to them, but no one knows."

"We must give him some of our time, although it seems he just isn't with us."

"He was a painter you know. Even in the Royal Gallery."

"Put the radio on – it may soothe him. I love this tune, oh look! Look at his face…"

Tilly, its your song. I can see you now, sunlight in your hair. I never captured you in oils, instead I set you free. Oh wait for me Tilly, this time let me dance too.

MOLLY'S SHOES

I didn't know why I had come. It was one of those dangerous times in my life when I stopped and wondered. Where am I going? What is it all for? I had a feeling of something missing. "Life in the West Riding". When I first saw this trip advertised for my study-group, I felt that I could escape for three weeks to somewhere I'd never been.

The group had visited museums, churches and schools. We had come to the last two days of our busy schedule. I was now free with a little cash in my pocket to wander around a small Northern town. Row upon row of the same red-bricked terraces stood like dominoes in a uniform parade. An old church charred with soot waited with an open door at the end of the row, the gravestones toppled with age, too black to show their names. Several miners waited at the bus-stop sitting on their heels joking and sparring with each other. Sunlight danced a morse-code in their lamps as they nodded and turned their heads.

As I turned, I saw a pub with its walls of olive-green tiles painted with golden scrolls. I stopped in my tracks and felt a warm sensation of belonging. I knew just around the corner were two rows of cottages, different from all the others. Slowly I tiptoed so as not to burst the bubble of hope and smiled with wonder. Two rows of yellow-stoned cottages facing inward to a short cobbled yard and I knew every inch of this road. It was Melba Place, my home, my world I knew so well. But how could this be? I had never been here before. I remembered feeling the cobbles piercing through red strappy girls' sandals. I stared at the clock-shaped drain where my doll's pram wheels had gotten stuck. I knew the house. It was at the end. The only one with a side entrance. I remembered playing cricket there with my brothers. Dad had moaned when we slammed the back door as it woke him after a night shift.

I squeezed my fingers into a fist to see if my nails pierced the flesh. Yes, I was awake, really here. I stopped outside the house, number twelve. I wanted to walk away – then some part of me was tempted to tread further, rap the knocker and wait. No one answered. I suppose in many ways I was relieved. What would I have said? As I was turning away, under a bush I saw a pair of women's shoes, and a note. I lifted the shoes and opened the note:

"Dear Molly,

Sorry to miss you. I had your shoes mended. Bert says they're past it, can't be heeled again. See you tomorrow.

Love Gran."

The shoes were old black slip-ons with a dusty bow, worn by a person who worked and needed to. With them still in my hands, a neighbour came out of her door and said,

"Hello Molly love. Shame you missed Doris, still it shouldn't be long 'till you'll be collecting Ian from school."

She left me speechless as she walked hurriedly away down Melba Place. I didn't know her. She'd thought I was Molly who wore these shoes – old fashioned, out of date and out of time, just as I felt as I stood at the door of a place I that knew to be home.

I walked away, past the corner where I remembered spending pocket money on *Iced-Gems*, then on to the school where I stood with mothers waiting for their children. At last the teachers brought them out and waited for them to be collected.

I knew which one was Ian, blond hair and large blue eyes like mine. He was chatting to a friend. I leaned forward. The teacher smiled at me and nodded for him to go. He stared at me and with a fear stricken face he slid behind the teacher's skirt and hid his head in the folds. A woman with a headscarf pushed in front of me. She called:

"Come on Ian, love."

He peeped, and with utter relief ran to her. I couldn't see her face but saw the wonderful way she engulfed the child in a loving hug. She held a well used wicker basket and in it were some old sandals. On her feet were the black, mended shoes with the dusty bow. I backed away as I saw the child pointing into the crowd trying to tell her something. She soothed him by rubbing his soft fair hair. I sidled away quickly, a trespasser.

I've never been back to my Northern town. What drew me there I will never understand. Yet, now I feel the warmth I would have known if I had been in Molly's shoes.

SWEET LILLIES OF EASTER

Up, up, up, one foot in front of the other, I pounded dusty boots in regular rhythm which kept me walking up the steep winding road. My rucksack was cutting sharply into my shoulders. The pain caused a light-headed feeling of not belonging anywhere. The sea mist swirling gave a hazy half light. I was so tired. I was no longer an angry man. The harsh words of the quarrel ceased their chanting. All I could think of was rest.

Through the mists I found mud tracks leading into a field. Pushing open the old wooden gate I could hear the sheep, but the mist was so dense I could see only a short distance in front of me. I sat on the damp soft grass and took off my heavy backpack. Soon I would put up my tent, but at this moment I felt that I would never summon up the energy to move again. Leaning back I closed my tired eyes and rested my head on the canvas bag.

I am not sure how long that I was lying there but I became aware of a lamb bleating for its mother. A high pitched pitiful call not far from where I lay. Was it caught in the wire fence or in the brambles of the hedge? I was just going to search for the poor creature when I heard the most beautiful sound. It was a woman's soft voice, as sweet and smooth as honey. It had a caring warmth which stirred the memory of being once loved by those I had just left. Over and over again, she said:

"Don't worry my love, Lilly's come. There there, I think it's time for you to go home."

The soft repeated murmurs seemed to spring new life within me. I peered through the haze to find her. As she murmured, "There there," and hummed a haunting melody, I saw what looked like movement through the mist. At first, her feet walking with care as she carried the lamb, now subdued. As she came closer I saw a radiance surrounding her every movement. Her soft diaphanous dress floated around her slender body. Long blond hair fell and curled about her tender white shoulders.

She didn't appear to notice me but petted and fussed the lamb, as a baby to her breast.

"There now you do as Lily says. You go, find your mother. You're safe now."

She put the lamb down and it gambolled away. She was so close, I felt as if I could touch her, but instead, in a voice unfamiliar to me, I croaked:

"Hello, is this your field?"

She didn't seem startled. It was as if she knew me and we had planned to meet.

"I suppose you might say it's mine, but if you need to rest it can also be yours for a while."

"I'd like to camp here."

She smiled a faint, knowing smile which I felt as a warm soothing balm healing all the wounds of the past few hours. She sat by my side, just the two of us in the deep dense mist as the evening shadows encircled our bodies.

She was perfection and I felt awkward at first in her presence. I stared into her glistening eyes. She understood, she knew I had left them. Never before had I felt so at one with another person. I knew Lilly was supreme and all else insignificant and lost. She gently held my hand and rested her head on my shoulder as we lay down in the soft dewy grass. Her soft hair brushed my cheek and her perfume of sweet hyacinths filled my body with a oneness which cocooned us in the stillness of time.

Perhaps it was a bird which woke me suddenly the next morning. I sat up with a start. A bright, sunny daylight, yet I was cold and alone. My lips shaped her name but she had gone. I was sitting next to the closed gate and sheep and lambs were scattered in the field. Some lambs were feeding, pulling and demanding, wriggling their tails. Others danced to keep up with their playmates.

I heard voices of people walking up the road. I felt like a trespasser and peeped through a hole in the fence. At first I thought it was her but it was a young woman who looked similar with a little girl by her side. They were smartly dressed with floppy hats. The child carried an enormous Easter egg. I remembered what day it was.

"Mum why did you buy a lilly and why did the vicar read out her name from the scroll?"

"It's to remember your nanny at Easter."

I heard the break in the young woman's voice and sensed her head was dipped to hide her eyes.

"What was she like, Mummy?"

"She was beautiful, like you darling."

The little girl beamed with pride, kicked up her feet and danced alongside her mother, like the lambs in the field.

They were gone as quickly as they had come. I ran to the gate and saw at the bottom of the hill a small church surrounded by haphazard graves and speckled daffodils.

I found myself walking down the hill to the church. Its door creaked open to show a celebration of gold and white. The altar held a large brass vase containing pure white lilies. They stood boldly on cloth with a lamb embroidered in golden thread. To my right was a wooden lectern with a parchment scroll. There were several names on the list but my eyes fell upon *Lilly Wainwright*.

I felt soft hair brush my hands and thought I could detect a hint of sweet hyacinth in the air. Again a soft voice whispered,

"Don't worry my love, Lilly's come. There there, I think it's time for you to go home."

DEEP WATERS RUN STILL

I woke up with a start. Sitting bolt upright like a puppet whose strings were jerked suddenly. I stared into darkness.

My wife slept soundly beside me. Her hair tussled, arms in abandoned semaphore signals, with a face so tranquil. She always was beautiful, even more so now she was pregnant.

"Don't you want your breakfast?"

"No thanks love. I had that dream again,"

I'm walking up a steep bank. Reaching the top I look down to a wide valley, and a solitary cottage, white with blue wooden shutters. Two small fir trees stand either side, near the edge of a smooth round lake. Two children are playing with a ball, dressed as if it were a hundred years ago. A lovely little girl and boy with golden curls.

Suddenly the girl, backing up to catch the ball, falls into the lake, screaming. The boy yells as I run with heavy feet. It's too late. The lake is black, deep, silent and empty.

The underlying sense of unease is gently mellowed by the days that pass.

"Darling we really must make up our minds. I like Darren or perhaps John? John is such a solid sort of name. Perhaps I ought to get one of those books?"

"She's going to be a girl," I said simply.

"How can you be so sure?"

"I've just got a feeling. I know her name too. Rosalind."

"A bit old fashioned. Why Rosalind? It's not one of your past girlfriends is it?"

"No, it just came to me. Rosalind feels right somehow."

"I don't dislike it, but he's going to be a boy!"

She was wrong. Our lovely little Rosalind was born two months later. I really regret not being there when she arrived but it was the day of my interview. I was trying for a headmaster's post at a village school near Dartmoor.

It had sounded idyllic but I'd not realised how remote it was. In the end I was surprised but thrilled to get the position. I could also have the school cottage at a low rent. We were invited to see it a week later.

It was a fair walk to the top of the hill past the sign to the school cottage. They had told me it had not been used for a few years and would need some work. Our little Rosalind cradled in cumbersome carrycot.

My wife ran ahead.

"Oh it's wonderful!"

It was all she'd ever wanted.

Eventually I got to the top of the hill. To my horror I saw the cottage from my dream. Now overgrown, the shutters unhinged and the fir trees twice the size. My eyes were drawn fearfully to the deep, black, silent, empty lake.

My wife began to run down the hill.

"Be careful!" I shouted. I tried to walk faster too, while keeping the carrycot level.

As she arrived at the lake I saw her suddenly stop. Next to the water's edge we saw a small stone pillar.

"To our darling daughter Rosalind. 1891-1897"

TO PEP YOU UP

It's happening again. I'm pouring water over more leaves for yet another cup of tea. I'll prepare the tray as always with polished cups and present it with a here it is smile. It's five to five. We always have tea at five o'clock. I hesitated and looked out of the window to the bleak winter night, misty and white with frost. No-one walked the lane now. All sensible homes were closing their blinds, sitting by the fire or boiling the kettle for yet another cup of tea.

I walked into the sitting room carrying the tray in my normal manner and placed it on the glass-topped table in front of his chair. I waited, he lowered the paper, looked over his half moon spectacles and then said, as always:

"Ah, nothing like a cup of tea to pep you up."

We had continued with this charade for almost twenty years and at this moment it felt like twenty decades rather than two. Suddenly my throat seemed to close and I clenched my teeth tightly. I held my breath and walked straight from the room.

I don't know exactly what happened to me but it was as if a band which held me together was being pulled too tight. Grabbing my coat I ran out the front door. The cold air rushed at my face and my pounding breath disappeared into the mist. My legs, as if they had only been made for this purpose, took me down lanes to my lonely spot by the canal. There was a bench where I had brought a picnic during long summer days. This place seemed alien now. Shadowed from a single lamp on the bridge, my lonely bench a damp, dark gravestone, flowerless and barren.

I walked to the bridge, leaned over and with cold hands gripped its smooth iced wood. All was silent and still. Dark shadows painted nighttime shapes clouded in some parts by a creeping mist. It was then I heard the soft licking of oars, rhythmically rippling the water. I saw a small rowing boat just below me. A bent figure in an overcoat steered to the edge and secured it. He climbed up the bank to the bench and sat with hands on knees. He looked at the bridge as if he knew I was there and said:

"I thought you'd come."

Strangely the old boatman did not frighten me. He had a curly mop of hair and an unkempt beard. Bony hands emerged from half fingered gloves. He was better wrapped for the cold than I was, but I warmed to his smile. He looked like a school boy who had just won his first game of marbles. I came down from the bridge to the tow path.

"How d'you know me?" I stammered. "How did you know I would be here?"

He just smiled and said, "Come with me."

Hypnotised, I followed him along to a stile, and climbed over. A path took us through the mist. All was silent.

I can't even remember the sounds of our shoes crunching the frost – hard stones of frozen earth. I could just see the outline of the cottage. I had walked these fields many times but never seen this. The cottage looked derelict with empty windows and dark outlined roof strangely squashed. Through a familiar creaking door I followed kicking and tripping over a clutter of abandoned bricks until we came to a small homely room.

When he lit the fire it flickered and the walls came to life. Several layers of paper were visible, with one patch of pink that I knew. It had silver squares with roses accurately duplicated in lines. I remembered as a child counting the blooms in the idle summer evenings before the pretty maids were diluted by the thin grey then black of the night.

The black clippy rag mat where we sat was similar to the one we had by the side of the tin bath when I was a child. I remembered how wonderful it felt to be warm and clean in a flannelette nightie, toasting the palms of my hands by the fire and scrunching toes into the grooves between the raggy gathers of the old bathtime mat.

I watched him boiling a billy-can on the fire. I felt no fear, just complete contentment at the warmth and a feeling that at last I had come home.

He poured the tea into some cracked cups with a worn picture of a Spanish lady painted on them. The lady smiled a sickly smile, unkind and glaring, incongruous in the warm peaceful surroundings. The tea was hot, strong and soothing. He cradled his cup then looking at me and with a smile he said:

"Nothing like a cup of tea to pep you up!"

I stood up, jerked into reality.

Again my throat seemed to close and with teeth clenched I dropped the cup and it smashed on the fender into the hearth. Once more the band within pulled all the sinews of my body tight.

I sprang from the room and dashed out into the cold air of night. I ran first to the stile, then the bench following the tow path to the bridge. My heart raced in rhythm with my pounding legs down the lane back to my front door.

As I opened the door I heard the clock strike five. I gingerly entered the sitting room and there was my husband with half a cup of tea in his hand and an unblemished smile. Next to his chair was a box of things wrapped in newspaper.

"What are these?" I asked.

"Well I found them on the step. P'raps they're for your jumble sale on Saturday?"

Unwrapping the first piece of crockery, pulling newspaper aside, and saw the sickly grin of the Spanish Lady.

I took a staggered step back. My husband looked up.

"You look worn out love. Sit down here, have a drink. There's nothing like a cup of tea to pep you up."

THE DAFFODIL SEASON

Every year I said it would be the last time. But here I am walking down the garden path with a wooden sign in my hand: "*Daffodil Cottage*. Bed and Breakfast."

Anyone seeing the garden now would know the reason for the name. I like them in rows. When their heads rise to the sun they remind me of chorus girls that danced at the old *Hippodrome* that was now rotting at the end of the pier.

I had a strange feeling someone was looking over my shoulder. I turned round, and saw a short, grey haired withered man. His clothes were as black as his face was white. He was carrying a black hand-painted wooden box by its handle and a small over-night bag. He lifted his hat and bowed stiffly.

"Excuse me Madam," he pronounced, "may I have a single room for a week?"

I had no reason to refuse as he had seen the sign and he gave me cash in advance.

As I showed him into the blue room, I began to feel uncomfortable letting this man into my home.

Later as he was leaving for his walk, I attempted to find out more about him.

"Have you been to Selcombe before, Mr Smith?"

"No." A short definite reply.

"Well as I don't provide an evening meal, may I recommend *The Old Bell* on the prom."

"That's the one next to the *Winter Gardens*?"

"Yes, but I thought you said…"

Before I could finish he had left the front gate walking with purpose as the wooden box rocked in his hand. He returned later that evening, went to his room and locked the door. As I was going to bed I thought I heard voices in his room. There was no television, no phone. He couldn't have anyone there because I saw him come in alone.

Intrigued I listened at the door. His voice was angry.

"I won't walk there again. I want to give it up, Elsie."

Then a high shrill voice,

"Yes you will dear but not just yet. It's only a gentle stroll to the end of the pier, to remember."

"You always say that. I want to give it up Elsie. I must."

"Of course dear, in time, of course. Get to sleep love, to be fit for the morning."

It was when I was collecting his breakfast things that I noticed it had gone. I had put a small daffodil in a short glass vase. It was now empty. I felt peeved at the trivial theft, though I could easily replace it.

My old cleaning lady Mrs Tibbett had passed him as he left the cottage.

"I know him," she said, "They used to live locally. He starred at the old *Hippodrome* years ago with his wife. She was a beautiful creature with golden ringlets and a red satin dress. Randall was their name as I remember. A magic act. Rather unusual because she did the tricks and he was her assistant. They came every year 'till she died. He tried a different act but was laughed off the stage."

"He told me his name was Mr Smith and he's never been to Selcombe before."

"Well he's a liar then. Never forget a name or a face."

That morning, the old vicar came with his monthly pack of magazines for me to distribute. He looked as if he had something on his mind, so I asked him if all was well."

"I've got a problem. Flowers have disappeared from the altar and some of the graves. It's most strange, only the daffodils were taken. Why should anyone do it?" My eyes were drawn to the short glass vase on my window sill.

"Vicar, have you heard of the Randalls?"

"Yes the wife is buried in the churchyard. She was a beautiful lady. They performed on the pier."

When Mr Smith returned that night he looked different. Brighter, happier and without a black box.

As he bid me goodnight, I noticed mud from his boots trailing in the carpet. There were no voices that night.

I called him the next morning, to no reply. After several attempts for an answer, I unlocked the door and found him gone. A neat blue room looking as though it had not been used. I felt relief but sensed a sudden chill. I decided to go for a walk as my little cottage seemed overwhelming.

As I shut the front door, I saw them. Neat rows of bare stalks. Every one of the golden heads was gone. I ran to the back lawn to see more naked green sticks. My legs walked with a mind of their own while infuriated tears ran down my cheeks. I went straight to the vicarage. The vicar talked in his usual calm manner but I was far from forgiveness. As I left, he pointed to a gravestone.

"The one at the end is Elsie Randall"

We walked over to the grave, surrounded with daffodils. Before I had chance to read the inscription the vicar said,

"What's this?"

With disbelief he pointed to a small neat, newly dug mound at the side of the headstone. The vicar ran to the vestry for a spade and began to dig. Soon the blade knocked against a box. It was the small black box with the handle. As we opened the lid we saw the daffodils. I thought it was full of them until I pulled back the blooms. It was then we saw the unhinged gape on the carved face of a ventriloquist's dummy, wearing an exquisite red satin dress, and with perfect golden ringlets.

From a Child's Point of View

JOSH

Why is it that whenever I see a lonely seagull dipping its wing in a clear blue sky, I want to close my eyes and whisper his name?

It was early morning when most sane folks are still in bed, I had driven there to breathe some fresh sea air. The beach and the prom were deserted. The tourist shops and arcades were closed. The large ice-cream parlour with its padded plastic pews stood in redundant dust and emptiness except for a dog-eared menu and a plastic cup of flat lemonade.

I had decided to walk down the stone steps to the beach. With a familiar whiff of salty spray, I knelt to gather pebbles and throw them into the waves of chanting sea. Then I sensed someone was watching me. I turned and saw those young dark brown eyes piercing from his sallow, unwashed face. He was huddled in a nook of the breakwater, turning pebbles in his hand.

"Oh! Hello," he had made me jump. "I didn't think anyone would be here."

"What you staring at Missus?"

"Nothing."

I lied. I knew what it was – those knowing eyes, with a depth of wisdom come too soon for a boy of his age.

"How come a lad like you's down on the beach at this unearthly hour?"

"Waiting for the boats. They'll be loaded coming back from the wharf. Sprats, 'undreds of them. They fill barrels for the vans but drop some. Gotta fill the bag for Gran."

"Do you live near here?"

"'Till the picking starts. Caravan's in a lay-by up Lynbrook. Just me and Gran."

"D'you go to school?"

"No… hey, you ain't the law are you?"

"No, oh no. What's your name?"

"Josh."

"Well, may I come down the wharf to see the sprats?"

"Suit yourself."

From the edge of the wharf we saw the boats escorted by gulls swooping and screeching with a greed of anticipation. As the boats were moored I saw the damp stinking decks heaving with nets, ropes, men, but above all, the flapping silver sprats. As the men hauled the fish into the large metal barrels, the boy became as one with the ravenous gulls dipping and snatching their easy catch from those that dropped. With his bag full, we walked back to the beach together.

"Do you have friends round here Josh?"

"I got cousins, aunties. Travellers stick together, but there was a bust up so Gran took us away 'till the picking starts. We're okay... look, I got dinner ain't I?"

The next day I saw him coming back from the wharf proudly swinging his bag. He was alone again.

"What do you like to do? Any favourite games, or books?"

"Can't read."

"Can you write your name?"

"No."

With a piece of driftwood I wrote "Josh" in the damp sand. He was stared at the name as I took his hand and helped him write over the letters. He was absorbed by this gesture. I took my diary and ripped out a few pages from the back. I wrote his name on the first sheet and gave him the pencil and paper. He paused, inspired.

"One day Missus, I'll have loads of books." he blurted. "And I'll put my name in them too!"

"Good idea Josh."

I left him twisting the pencil in his hand with pride.

Work consumed me for a week or so and then I thought I'd better return home. I decided to go Lynbrook Way.

FROM A CHILD'S POINT OF VIEW

Perhaps I would see the caravan? At the bottom of the hill I was kept waiting behind traffic. I wound down the window to see cars at a standstill halfway up. I got out to see what was wrong. It was then I saw the caravan a burnt out wreck still smouldering at the side of the road.

A policeman was directing the cars.

I panicked. "Anyone hurt?"

"One old girl died before they got here, but the boy is okay. He's gone to Tineton for a full check up."

I drove to the hospital but I had missed him.

"They came to pick him up," the nurse said. "They made him leave this bag of old books."

"We don't nick things!" they had yelled at him.

I saw the books were all the same – a book of Common Prayer and Hymns with "Lynbrook Church" embossed on the front. I found the pencil lodged inside a cover and opening each book I saw in clear, bold and very proud print, the name "Josh."

THE BOOKMARK

At first Sir used to read out her name, then look around our faces. But now, he would pause and Lizzie Warren's name was not called.

She had not been at school long. They sat her in the empty space next to my desk. She had long lank hair and her faded dress hung on her. I had not liked her from the beginning because her neat sloped writing was full of ticks and stars. It was as if her dip pen never blotted. Her desk was as tidy as a library shelf.

She had been absent from school for weeks now. At first I used to kick her neatly embroidered dap bag until it rocked and twisted on her peg, but it saddened me now. I had taken some new crayons from her pencil tin as mine were worn. I'd borrowed her rubber then decided to keep it.

I knew it was stealing.

My Dad always said "Know what is your own."

I really wanted to take the dried-flower bookmark with the golden tassel but instead I lifted the lid of her desk and each day took a peep.

She lived in an old converted shop, a bookies with the large windows painted opaque green. It had a brass handled door, that I had knocked to see if Lizzie was coming to school soon – no reply.

Her next door neighbour was scrubbing her step.

"They're not in. Went out early this morning. Probably at the hospital. Lizzie's been getting worse."

I ran to the corner shop to buy a bag of gums with the threepence burning in my pocket. I would not eat them today. I would take them to the hospital, share them with Lizzie. Ask her to be my friend.

I knew the Children's Ward from when I'd broken my arm. In twos, I climbed the steps to the Sister's desk. When I asked to see Lizzie she hesitated and looked uncomfortable. She smiled too much and showed me into an empty waiting room with comics. I saw some roses in a vase and wished I'd asked my Dad for some from home. Then Sister Morris came in. She had been kind to me when she bandaged my arm.

"You've come to see Lizzie Warren?"

"Yes," I answered simply, "she's my friend. Sits next to me in school. I brought her some gums."

"Lizzie is not here any more. I want you to go home to your mother for your tea,"

"Where is she? Is she better? Can I give them to her?"

She stopped, put her arm around my shoulder and with a voice no louder than a whisper,

"I'm sorry dear, Lizzie was very ill. Go home to Mum."

Oh no, she couldn't be...

All that filled my mind was her neat sloping handwriting and rows of ticks. I'd never actually spoken to her, but I wanted so much to speak to her now.

I heard my mother's worried whispers. It was a week before I returned to school. It was decided that I should go into my brother's class with the younger children, just for a while. As days passed I still saw her face.

One evening, after the end of day bell I crept back into the old classroom to return Lizzie's crayons and rubber to her desk. Bravely I opened the wooden lid to see someone else's books. Then I realised that all the desks had been moved around. The crayons and rubber grew hot in my hand. How could I give them back?

Aimlessly I wandered into the playground. It was then I smelled the rubbish burning. The caretaker was loading the spoils of the week into a low metal barrel. The red coals in the centre warmed my face.

As he poured on another sackful of old papers and exercise books, I saw her name in neat sloping hand.

There were Lizzie's books. Burning with the rubbish.

My eyes caught the shimmer of a golden tassel. It was the bookmark. I screamed at the caretaker,

"It's the bookmark! The flower bookmark!"

I panicked him into action and he managed to grasp it before it fell into the flames. The first tears fell silently as he gently laid the golden tassels between my fingers.

"Here you are," he said kindly, "you have it."

Through a cloud of tears I whispered, "I can't".

I heard Dad's voice. "Know what is your own."

I took the crayons, rubber and lastly the golden tasselled bookmark and threw them back where they belonged, with all that was left for me of Lizzie Warren.

GOLDEN SANDS TO GREY

If I close my eyes I can still feel my feet in sandy plimsolls pounding down the well worn paths between the knee high bracken. I felt that this haven of summer days could never be touched with fear until one year when for a while, the golden sands turned grey.

We had wondered if the Barfields would hire the chalet next to us again. It was like ours, a wooden hut with a green painted veranda, faded curtains and a lop-sided sign. Ours was *Seaside Escape* theirs was *Byeways*. Their chalet was locked and unused when we arrived. I was disappointed. I was longing to see Marie. She was the same age as me and for the last two summers we had met and played on the dunes for hours.

Later that evening when it was dark I was listening to raindrops dancing on the roof. Then suddenly the small timbered room was lit up by headlamps of a car arriving next door. I peeped through the space where the curtains had shrunk and saw lights in Byeways' windows and Mr Barfield moving cases. They were back. I hugged my knees with excitement. I heard Dad go out to help carry luggage.

FROM A CHILD'S POINT OF VIEW

He was a long time and when he came back he was speaking to mum in a low serious tone. Something was wrong. I crept out of bed to listen at the door.

"He says she was deported last February. Her visa expired. A maid's salary was not enough."

Then Mum's voice, trembling, "Oh the poor little love, mother sent away, and only six years old."

I went back to my bunk, picked up my old teddy bear and hugged him hard. Mrs Barfield was a kind lady with a flowery apron and lovely accent. She always smiled at me and spoke in short, simple phrases. She had giggled with mum as they peeled potatoes on the veranda in the sun.

Questions filled my head. Who will cook the dinners? Who will wash her clothes? Who will stroke her hair and hold her tightly when bad dreams come?

Dads are great for piggy back rides and telling stories, or lifting high on their shoulders after washing your feet in rock pools. But, they always pull your socks on your feet when they are still damp and fasten sandal straps too tight

I couldn't bare to imagine life without a mum. I called out, and after soft reassuring words, I fell asleep in her arms.

The next morning, Mum said:

"Why don't you go and knock at their door? I'm sure Marie will want to come out and play. There's no need to mention it unless she wants to."

I saw her out by the car. She looked the same and yet there was a difference. We smiled and said hello and as we always had, we ran down the bracken-edged path to the beach. We carried our sandals.

The sand was warm and soft. We ran all the way to the shore and made new small prints in the damp firm sand. We collected limpet shells to rattle in our pockets and began a game of chase. I caught Marie and we bumped down to the ground exhausted.

Suddenly her face was serious and she whispered:

"My mum went back to France."

I just said, "Yes."

She got up calmly and stood facing the water. The red flags were flying. We knew that meant we mustn't bathe here. It was a dangerous spot where the river estuary met the sea. We stood near the edge skimming a few stray pebbles on the tempting waves and watched the curling foam rising and falling in time with the roar of the sea.

As we turned our back we heard voices from further down the beach. Some people were in the water, other were yelling and waving. One man came running up to us, shouting, panicked. I couldn't understand him but Marie started to answer in French.

"His wife is drowning! We've got to get help!"

We ran, my feet slipping ridiculously on the soft sand that only minutes before we had tumbled down with delight. The two dads were snoozing in deck chairs outside the chalets. My dad went to to phone for help. Marie's dad ran to the beach. We were told to stay in the chalet.

Mum put her arms around us and said how brave we had been. She kissed Marie's forehead and said how wonderful it was that she could speak French. Marie started to cry.

We slept head to toe in my narrow bunk that night. I felt like crying too but didn't know why. I let Marie have my best teddy to hold.

The next day the grown-ups planned a special day when we could all go to town to buy souvenirs then come back for a sunset picnic on the sand. We almost forgot the day before until Dad said:

"Now you girls be careful on the beach. The sea is powerful. The current is so strong."

Watching the last sun flickering, the sea turned black and cold. The sand, no longer golden became a cool steel grey.

GINNIE

Ginnie ran behind the shed and covered her ears to drown the thud of the heavy cleaver. Silence. Not a flap or a squawk, the chicken was dead. It was carried by its feet, limp and dripping to the shed. She ran to kneel at the chopping block. Her fingers traced the surface as tears joined the blood in the cruel grooves. It always felt wrong. To Ginnie this was violence and violence frightened her.

When she first came to Nan Price she was just six years old. A sad little girl who had bush baby eyes and white blond hair. She was a strange child. Around her, time had no meaning. That was ten years ago and although some claimed Ginnie was "not quite the ticket" she grew as an delicate wildflower in the tiny village of Ryanshall.

One day a van came down the muddy path to Nan's cottage. No-one owned a car in the village and few salesmen called at Ryanshall. The van was painted green with golden letters that Ginnie could not read. She was hiding at the side of the privy. A young man with curly hair and confident stride opened the back of the van.

The man had a large bicycle horn and it blasted through the silence of the valley. Nan came out of the cottage bewildered, disturbed from her after dinner nap.

"What is it? What is it?" she shouted.

"Hello Missus. My name is Jack Lloyd. I've come to see if there's anything you need. You look here Missus. Have you ever seen such a spread?"

He pulled back the van doors like a showman and proudly presented the goods. There were pots and pans; paint and tools; bright linen and gaudy mats; *Kilner* jars and curtain rings and much crockery crammed tightly to perfection to tempt the eye.

"Hey Ginnie, stop gawping girl. Go to the tea caddy on the mantelpiece, run!"

Nan's eyes settled on a gilt-edged vase with a delicate handle on either side. On the front there was a picture of a carthorse and plough. It reminded her of her father whose tired bones lay in the church yard. She had no photograph, but this could be a reminder of the days she would meet him with a bottle of cold tea and a chunk of bread. It was a lovely vase, kind to the eye and the memories would warm her on a cold winter evening.

"Ah I see you're taken by the vase, Missus. A bargain and lovely with flowers or without. Here, hold it."

She smoothed her palm over the generous belly of the vase. She wanted it. Perhaps it was the only frivolous buy she had ever made, but her father had left the cash, all notes still untouched, tacked to the bottom of the mattress. They were for Ginnie's future. The tea caddy money should just about cover it.

Cradling the vase with reverence she walked back to the cottage. But Jack did not close the van doors as he saw Ginnie come closer to take a look inside. As her eyes wandered over the goods his eyes wandered over Ginnie. He liked girls. He had known many, but none like her.

"Hello there," he said in a low gentle voice, "so you're Ginnie. I've never heard that name before."

"It's really Virginia, but Nan calls me 'Ginnie'."

"Is there just you and Nan?"

"Yes." He took out a small china brooch in the shape of a rose. "This is really pretty. D'you like it? Just right for you you to wear to market on your best coat."

"It's lovely. But I don't go to market. Nan goes every Wednesday while I stay home to get the dinner ready and feed the chickens."

"Oh that's too bad. Don't you go anywhere?"

"Well, I like the wood and walking the old railway line. The track is still there. You can go all the way to Ritley."

"Is there anything left there?"

"Old timetables and tickets scattered about, and dusty old railway coats hanging on the door."

"I'd like to go there," he said and she smiled. He stood there looking at her. She was so innocent, lovely and with such large open eyes.

He waved and got back into the van. Ginnie was sad to see him go. Would she see him ever again?

The next Wednesday as she was preparing the vegetables Ginnie heard the brass door knocker. She'd been told never to unlock the house but she recognised his voice as he gently called her name.

She gingerly opened the door.

"Sorry, Nan's not here."

"It's you I've come to see. I've got an hour or so free. Thought you might like to come out for a walk."

"I'd like that, but I don't know."

"What are you worried about? You're not scared of me surely. It's all right. I'll help you with your jobs first. Now go and put on your Sunday best and I'll wait here."

"But it isn't Sunday."

"Ah, but it's a special day. You can be my girl for the afternoon. Be quick!"

When she had left he looked around the meagre living room. A square table was covered with a red velveteen cloth. Grandad stood as a soldier in a wooden frame and watched from the wall. There were faded religious pictures and a tapestry claiming "Honesty is the Best Policy". He spotted the vase and smiled at the profit he had made on it. Where was the tea caddy? He spotted it, shook it. Empty. In a strange way he was glad.

He had known Ginnie was different but didn't realise how different until their walk in the woods. She ran down a well worn pathway to her "house" where she played there. A wooden box she called her stove was sat on the earthy ground. Around the stove were "tiles" of pieces of broken china. Fragments of willow pattern and red poppies placed together as a jigsaw puzzle with many spare parts. A rusty kettle with no bottom was perched on the stove. An up-turned tin bath covered by an old curtain was a settee. Under it she kept old catalogues, rescued from the tip.

She showed him pictures of beautiful houses and kitchens. These were her dreams. Sitting on the tin bath watching a kettle that would never boil he found it difficult to know what to say. Perhaps he shouldn't have come. He found the trust in her eyes unsettling.

"It's no use looking at these pictures Ginnie, all those things cost money. Lots of it. One day I want to own my own shop in a town. People will come to me, not me to them. But it takes a lot of money."

Ginnie whispered "Some people have lots of money, but they never spend it."

"What do you mean?"

"I shouldn't tell."

"You can tell me, we're friends. I won't tell a soul."

"Nan's got money…"

"Oh, I don't think so Ginnie. She doesn't seem well off."

"I saw her counting it. It's sewn to the bottom of the mattress. She said it was a secret to keep for a rainy day. There's been many stormy days but she hasn't touched it."

She stopped abruptly. "Nan's calling."

"Well before you go I've brought you something".

He placed in her hand the little rose brooch.

"I can't pay."

"No, It's a gift from me to say we're friends. Don't tell any-one. I'll meet you here, Wednesday at two o'clock."

He had hidden his van away from the house to avoid suspicion. He started to think of his own little shop, the one he had always dreamed of.

The next Wednesday at two o' clock Jack tiptoed into the cottage. It was so easy. The door was not even locked. Masses of notes in cloth bags were sewn to the bottom of the mattress. He filled his rucksack as fast as he could.

Jack thought of Ginnie waiting for him in the woods. He hadn't planned to actually meet her, but as he was about to drive past he found himself stopping.

"Oh Jack, I thought you weren't coming."

"Of course I'm here, aren't I? But we've got to be quick, very quick. Ginnie, I'm going to buy a little shop. You can help behind the counter. We'll live in the rooms above and decorate it just like your magazines."

"I can't come. Nan would worry."

He began to panic and raise his voice.

"D'you want to play pretend in this place all your life?"

Ginnie started to cry. "Don't shout at me. I'm no good in towns, or with people. I get frightened."

He grabbed her arm and she pulled away, suddenly remembering the chicken flapping, squawking on the block. She broke lose and ran as fast as she could back to the cottage. It was beginning to rain.

Nan found Ginnie slumped over the china brooch. She wouldn't say what was wrong. Taking her coat upstairs, Nan found the upturned mattress.

"The money's gone! Who took it Ginnie? And where did you get that brooch?"

Ginnie crouched down on the floor and hugged herself crying loudly. For the first time in many years Nan knelt and put her arms gently around to console her. She rocked her and stroked her hair.

Rain lashed against the window and Ginnie raised her eyes.

"Nan, is this is the rainy day we've been waiting for?"

GOTTA READ BY SPRING

"Look Miss, I've got to learn quick, not just signs and things, but big thick books, really read them. Learn me quick Miss – gotta read by spring."

Don had marched into my room and demanded this with his small round face so earnest. I didn't dare smile!

"Like your room Miss, pretty like. Can I have this book?"

"Wait a minute Don, let's find out a bit about you."

"I can read Miss, went to school once. D'you know Miss Robinson? Best teacher she was. But, we move around, see. That's why I gotta learn now."

I don't know what I'd expected, but Don wasn't it.

He had glossy hair and a toothpaste advert smile, designer jumper as well. He was cocky, his eyes bright and sharp. No-one would get the better of him.

At seven years old he could read his name, and "NO".

He was keen to learn more and would bargain with me:

"Hey Miss if I do this writing can I go out to play?" or "Miss, if I read down to there will you give me a star?".

He talked at a thousand miles and hour. "Who else d'you have in your little room? Do they read as good as me? If I learn real good I'll earn a hundred quid a week like Dad. See that playground out there? Well me Da' will tarmac it for a thousand quid, not a penny less, cheap at the price!"

Every day before settling down to read about *Peter and Jane* in their well ordered life, he'd chat to me about his own

"Well I gets the water for Mum, heavy it is but I can carry it. I brings it to our trailer. It's bigger than my cousin's. Got a stove and a chimney!"

"Does your mum work, Don?"

"Crikey yeah Miss. She sells peat and manure - £3.75 a bag. Gets it from the farms – pigs and sheep. One farmer tried to sell us goose manure. Ya can't have that, can ya? Mad he was. Hey Miss I know that word – it's 'shop'."

He pointed at the word "as".

"Well, I saw it on a shop once."

"I think you're right, Don. Was it *Asda*? That's a shop."

"You drive, Miss?"

"Yes, I've got a *Land Rover*."

"They're good they are. Pull a trailer good, four wheel drive. We've got three vehicles: a pickup, a red Volvo – a new one, don't carry peat in that, and the tarmac van.

It's got a light on the top. That's the tarmac sign. We've got planks to put the roller up and in the back there's brushes, shovels and spanners. Hey Miss, what's this?"

He was pointing to a zebra in a book about a zoo.

"Have you ever been to a zoo Don?"

"No Miss, but we goes to the races. I meet all my cousins there. I place me bet then we sit up in the tower and yell and yell! You get ice-creams and hot dogs there. You been to the races Miss?"

"No, never."

One day he was writing the first letters of words under a picture and I asked,

"You put an 'm' under a 'gun', is that what it starts with?"

"Well Miss, it's a *Magnum* isn't it. What's this?"

He pointed at a picture of a boy. "It's a Cubs uniform. I've got a picture of my son dressed as a Cub. Here it is."

"What do they do?"

"Well they learn to tie knots, play games, camp and build fires…"

"And they dress up to do *that?*"

As he learned, Don loved each new book. He would take them back to his trailer and proudly show his parents how to read the new words.

Don used to hide school notes in his drawer. Once he missed a trip because of this.

One day I said, "Don I think it would be a great idea if you could have your own book – all about you."

"Not with *Peter and Jane*?"

"Not this one. It's going to be about you and your family."

"You gonna make it Miss? Will it be printed like a real book? Gotta a typewriter Miss? We got one, but no one can write. I play on it sometimes."

"You can help me type it. Tell me what to write. You can draw the pictures. It'll be special. No-one will have a book like this one."

So each day we typed and drew to make Don's book. It was written simply so he could read it to everyone that visited his home. It was all about tarmac and peat, the races and the trailer, and the hope that one day he would own a scrambling bike like his cousin.

Sadly, the book lies unfinished in my room, in a drawer marked "Don". He left abruptly after about six weeks as soon as the warmer weather came.

Don's different way of life and fresh free spirit had taught me almost as much as he had learned. Our time together was brief, but I am pleased to say that he read by spring.

THE WISHING STONE

What was that? There was a rustle amongst the leaves. I turned to see a hawthorn bush wearing red sandals and wrinkled socks. I could see her dark eyes peering through and when she realised I had seen her she pushed the branches away and rather hesitantly came forward and sat a distance from me.

"Hello," I said with a hint of amusement.

"This is my place." She sounded peeved and hugged her dusty knees. She stared hard at me with piercing eyes.

"Are you going now?"

I felt reluctant to leave.

"Why should I?" I simply answered, "I hadn't planned to."

She screwed up her face as if she was resigned to ignore my presence and then took something out of her pocket.

It was a stone. She put it in her two hands with arms outstretched. Eyes tightly closed, and holding her breath, she raised her face to the sky.

"What are you doing?"

She didn't answer but frantically shook her head with annoyance, her bulging cheeks trying to keep hold of her breath. With an enormous burst of air she put the stone back in her pocket. In a matter of fact way she replied,

"I was using my wishing stone."

"Can I see it?"

She looked at me cautiously for a moment then took it out of her pocket. She held it out with care as if it were priceless. A smooth grey stone with a circle of pink grain.

"You see that," she said pointing to the circle, "that's the blood. When I hold it tight it warms up and the power goes up my arms to my head and I feel strong. Then I know the wish will come true."

"And it always works?" I asked solemnly, trying to be as earnest as she was.

"Well mostly," she replied, crestfallen.

"You mean it sometimes lets you down?"

"Sometimes."

We sat in silence for a moment. Then I said jokingly,

"What you need is a special mark on it."

Her eyes grew in wonder. I warmed to her interest.

"Yes, what you need is a magic W for 'wishes'."

She gave me the stone and with a pencil from my pocket I drew a small "W" on it.

"That will give it special strength" I smiled.

When I gave it to her, it was as if it were suddenly Christmas. Her face was a picture of hope. She held the stone out insistently to the sky and closed her eyes tightly.

"Please, please wishing stone let my Dad come back."

The smile fell from my face and yet the Christmas hope was still in hers. She jumped up impatiently and began to run away, but then she stopped and turned.

"Thanks Miss, Thanks a lot."

"Hey what's your name?"

"Amy Morgan!" she called, still running.

"Where do you live?"

"Above the Post Office."

And then she was gone.

I felt stupid and ashamed. Why did I spin her such a tale? I was so annoyed with myself I gritted my teeth and felt tears of frustration rising.

I had only meant it as a joke, but she believed every word.

For several days I felt unsettled, and although my friends told me to forget it, Amy's hopeful eyes still haunted me. I found myself walking to the Post Office.

Mrs Morgan opened the door. She was a woman worn with grief rather than age, a flat expressionless face.

"If you're selling I'm not buying, so leave me in peace."

"No, excuse me Mrs Morgan, it's about Amy."

"Is she alright?"

I began to tell her about the stone and all that happened. She was silent, saddened and with a tired voice said:

"I don't know of any old stone."

She stopped then led me to a chair. "See, Bill lost his job. It doesn't do for a man to be in all day. He stood it for a while but seemed to lose his pride. Took to going down *The Red Lion*, not often at first. I couldn't stop him. Lives somewhere in town. Don't know what we're going to do."

I felt useless as I gave her my name and address and lamely said to let me know if I could be of help. With hunched shoulders I walked home.

I had never been in a pub on my own before, certainly not one like *The Red Lion* but as the days went by I knew I had to talk with Bill Morgan, for Amy's sake. I stole courage to enter and the stench of stale beer filled my nostrils.

"Please can you tell me if Bill Morgan is here?"

The greasy bar tender raised an eyebrow and I could see he was reading something lurid into the situation.

FROM A CHILD'S POINT OF VIEW

"Hey Bill there's a young lady to see you."

He stumbled over, spilling his beer as he walked. With half opened eyes he stared blankly at me.

"I'm sorry to disturb you Mr Morgan."

"What do you want?" He was tired and aggressive.

"It's about Amy. She misses you."

"What's it to do with you?"

Then I told him about the stone. He stood listening and when I had finished he put the glass on the bar. He slumped on the stool and said with a faint smile:

"I remember that stone. It was on holiday last year. She saw it in a rock pool. Looked real pretty when it was wet. When it dried in the sun it grew dull. She was disappointed so I told her that when I was a kid I had a wishing stone. Never thought it would come to this."

He looked into his glass and I felt he didn't want me there.

A few days later I found a small parcel left on my front doorstep. It was badly wrapped in Christmas paper and inside I found the wishing stone and a crumpled note.

In a child's bold print it read:

"You have it, we don't need it now."

Bing-Bing Stories

Illustrations in pencil & ink by my son Sam, the original "Victor".

VICTOR MEETS BING-BING

Have you ever noticed that truly wonderful things can happen when you are least expecting them? This was certainly true of the day Victor found Bing-Bing.

Mum, Dad and Victor had taken a trip in the car one Saturday afternoon. Just by chance they had found a small fairground. They had thought it would be a treat but everything seemed to be going wrong. The fire engine ride had been a disaster – the bell hadn't worked. Victor had thrown a ring and missed the peg so he did not win a goldfish. The waltzers looked very exciting but Mum said they were a "big boy's ride", and now they were going home with miserable faces.

Then Dad spotted the coconut shy. He said he would try and knock down six. He managed three and the man pointed to a frayed old box full of cheap plastic toys.

Among them was a dusty cuddly penguin. Victor could not stop looking at his sad eyes. Then he thought he saw his little orange felt beak bob up and down.

A baby in another mum's arms called out "Bing-Bing!" and everyone laughed.

"It's not bing-bing it's penguin," corrected the mum but Victor decided it was a lovely name. He pointed to him so Dad took Bing-Bing out of the box and Victor met him for the first time.

He held him tightly all the way home in the car and when they stood outside the front door Dad started patting his pockets and muttering cross words.

Where's the key? He kept saying.

Bing-Bing's beak started bobbing up and down and it pointed towards the car. Victor ran to the car door and saw the keys on the floor by the back seat!

"They're here Dad" he shouted.

"Well what a clever lad," Dad said patting Victor's head. Victor was just going to say it was Bing-Bing who knew where they were when something in the little penguin's eyes told him not to say a word.

As Bing-Bing was rather dirty Mum said she would wash him very carefully. After a splash in the wash bowl and a twirl in the spin dryer Bing-Bing looked a little flat and his fur was squashed but Mum said if he danced in the warm air of the tumble dryer he'd be a really beautiful penguin.

It was true. His shining button eyes sparkled. His little penguin wings were fluffy and floppy, and he seemed to push out his now snowy-white breast with pride.

Victor took him upstairs to his bedroom. He showed Bing-Bing his frog mobile, his train set, still left out in the corner and lastly introduced him to Edward Bear who was sitting up in a dimple on the pillow.

"Edward this is Bing-Bing," announced Victor. He pressed their noses together in a kiss and something told him that this was only the beginning of their adventures.

BING-BING AND THE CARAVAN

There was once a boy called Victor who had a teddy bear called Edward and a furry toy penguin whose name was Bing-Bing. As soon as Victor found Bing-Bing he knew that he was no ordinary cuddly toy. He was very special.

Victor had always longed to sleep in a caravan. He had seen them at the sea-side so he was thrilled when Dad said he had bought one.

"It's only an old one," he had said, "it used to be a snack bar near the motorway but with a little bit of work we'll have it fit for a holiday."

That weekend Dad peeled off the sticky letters saying "Snack Bar" and took out all of the old boxes of stale crisps and flat lemonade.

Victor took Bing-Bing into the caravan and they both huddled in a corner inside a sleeping bag, eating a fresh bag of crisps – cheese and onion, his favourite! Victor put one crisp on Bing-Bing's felt beak, then ate it for him.

Mum was putting up some pretty new curtains made from bedspreads and laying bright new pieces of carpet. It was a lovely holiday home and Victor could hardly wait to live in it. It was springtime and not very warm but all the family decided they couldn't wait 'til summer to try the caravan.

"We'll go down to Doug's farm near *Sandy Bay*," Dad said and Mum began to pack.

It was a long journey and when they arrived they found an empty field with just a few sheep and their lambs dotted about the grass. It was getting dark and a sea mist started to circle around the caravan.

Victor had brought Edward Bear and Bing-Bing of course. Mum tucked Victor into the sleeping bag on the lower bunk and kissed him goodnight, but he just could not get to sleep. The wind was blowing around the caravan and it seemed to rock and creak.

He must have slept for a little while but he suddenly woke up with a start. Bing-Bing was struggling in his arms and rubbing his little felt beak up and down on Victor's cheek.

"What is it Bing-Bing?" he whispered.

"Bing-Bing's beak pointed to the window. Victor opened the curtain and felt a sudden bump at the side of the caravan, then he heard a high pitched crying sound. It was all too frightening so Victor shouted, "Dad!"

Dad fumbled for his torch. Wearing pyjamas and wellingtons, he went out into the darkness.

"It's alright," he shouted, "it's only a sheep trying to rescue her lamb, he got stuck under the van." Bing-Bing's beak nodded frantically but Victor stroked him reassuringly.

After much persuading Dad carefully lifted out the lamb and it danced back to its mother. When he came back into the caravan Dad was covered in mud. Mum laughed and said she would make hot chocolate for everyone.

"I'm hungry," said Victor.

"You're always hungry!" Mum replied and she hunted for some biscuits.

Victor looked to see why Bing-Bing was shuffling about in the sleeping bag and right by his hand he found a cheese and onion crisp. Victor munched it secretly.

"It was a good job you heard that little lamb, Victor. He was really frightened," Dad said proudly.

Victor was just about to say it was Bing-Bing who had woken him when something in the furry penguin's eyes told him not to say a word. So he smiled and picked up Edward Bear and Bing-Bing and pressed their noses together in a kiss. With one under each arm he drifted at last into a warm happy sleep.

BING-BING AND THE PENGUINS

There was once a boy called Victor who had a teddy bear called Edward and a furry toy penguin whose name was Bing-Bing. As soon as Victor found Bing-Bing he knew that he was no ordinary cuddly toy. He was very special.

Since Bing-Bing had joined the family Victor had started asking lots of questions about penguins. He had never actually seen one in real life, only in books about zoos, so Mum and Dad decided to take Victor to *Birdland*.

Victor hugged Bing-Bing under his arms as Mum paid for the tickets to go in. There were so many birds. Some bright screechy ones, others delicate and shy.

Victor huddled up to his Mum when an owl stared at him with large round eyes. Dad was pointing out the nesting boxes where the budgerigars hatched their eggs but Victor kept tugging and looking around to find the penguins.

At last they came to a large pool with glass at the one side so everyone could see the penguins on top and swimming under the water. Victor stared in amazement with his nose squashed against the glass. The penguins swam so easily as if they were flying and drawing shapes under the water with their heads. Then they would flop out like a lump of jelly and stand still and proud on the cold wet shore. Victor held Bing-Bing up to show him.

"These are your long lost cousins Bing-Bing," he whispered. Bing-Bing's eyes sparkled as if he knew already. A tall man wearing a rubber bird-keeping apron and green wellingtons came to the side of the pool carrying a bucket full of fish. As soon as he came the penguins waddled up to him and gathered round to wait impatiently.

He fed the large penguins one by one, each fish swallowed whole. He threw some small fish into the pool and the younger penguins dived in each wanting to get there first.

Victor climbed up a bank to see more but as he was doing so he felt Bing-Bing shuffling under his arm. He seemed to be looking towards the other side of the pool. His little orange beak was bobbing up and down alarmingly. Victor knew there was something wrong and forgetting his mother's instructions to stay close to them he ran around the side of the pool to a fenced area.

One little penguin so eager to hop out the water for his fish had landed next door in the goose pen. The harsh beaky white geese were all around him squawking. The poor little penguin crossed his wings over his chest and bent his head in fright. Bing-Bing's beak moved frantically.

"Don't worry Bing-Bing we'll get him out," said Victor and ran back to the poolside to tell his Mum and Dad.

Mum was just about to scold him for running away when Victor told them about the poor little penguin. Dad ran around to see and soon caught the attention of the keeper throwing the fish. When the little penguin was picked up in the strong arms of the man Victor cheered and hugged Bing-Bing tightly.

When they got home, Mum stood puzzled.

"What I don't understand is how did you know the little penguin needed to be rescued?"

Victor was just going to say it was Bing-Bing who had found him, when something in the little penguin's eyes told him not to say a word.

"Well, Edward Bear has been waiting long enough for you to come to bed. Edward, do you know that Victor was a hero today? He saved a little penguin."

Victor put Bing-Bing next to Edward and pressed their noses together in a kiss.

He whispered so that only they could hear:

"It wasn't me, it was Bing-Bing. He's the real hero."

ACKNOWLEDGEMENTS

Many of the stories in this book have been published
or broadcast over the years, including:

- *You Deserve Better*   *BBC Radio,* & several magazines
- *Six Mince Pies*   *BBC Radio,* & adapted into a musical
- *Just a Bit of Fun*   *BBC Radio*
- *The Primrose Line*   *BBC Radio*
- *Gloucester's Child*   *Cotswold Life* magazine,   October 1991
- *Gotta Read by Spring*   *Cotswold Life* magazine,   January 1992
- *The Wishing Stone*   *Candis,* Volume 3 Issue 12,   November 1988

Ann is a four-time selection for *The Times* and *The Sunday Times* Cheltenham Literature Festival through *Gloucestershire Writers' Network*. The stories *Olé Olé Olé* and *Talbot Way* were selections, along with *Gloucester Ghosts Walk* from her anthology *Every Poem has a Story*, and *My Dad, a Man of Few Words* from her autobiography *A Wealth of Pennies*.

Her poetry was featured on *ITV*'s *TV-AM* during the 80s, and religious songs that she has written have been featured on radio, television and newspapers, now compiled in *Songs to Make a Difference*. All of the above mentioned books are all available worldwide on *Amazon, Kindle, Audible*, and from independent retail outlets, published by *Victorious MCG*.

∞⁂∞

Over the years Ann's stories and poetry have been published in many anthology books and magazines alongside other writers, including:

- *Celebration*   *Dean Writer's Circle*   ISBN 9781739787417
- *Forest Leaves 5*   *Dean Writer's Circle*   ISBN 9780953547371
- *High Spots*   *Anchor Books*   ISBN 1859301142
- *Write to the Edge Again* *B.R.*   ISBN 0952241811
- *Ad-Lib: Short Story Magazine 2* *BookWorms*
- *Pause.. No 31*   *National Poetry Foundation*
- *Pause.. No 32*   *National Poetry Foundation*
- *Just Words*   *Gloucester Writer's Circle*
- *Celebrating 10 Years*   *Gloucester Writer's Circle*
- *Poetry Anthology '88*   *A.E.W.*

The publishers of this book wish to gratefully acknowledge all of the publishers, broadcasters and writers groups mentioned, as well as Newhall Publications, L&C Communications, editors Elaine Harrison, John Drinkwater, David B. MacDonald, Jean Cooper Moran, Cheryl Mayo, Val Ormrod, Tony Wilde, Felicity Edwards, John Stanley, Michelle Abbot, Bryan Ricketts, Bob Jenkins, E.J. Bouchard, Alice Emelia Wilmshurst, and all who have supported and encouraged her writing over the course of her career.

A MUM OF MANY WORDS
Samuel Victor

When I was a child, my mum wrote a short story about her father, my grandfather Victor Leyfield, called *My Dad, a Man of Few Words*. This led to her being selected for a literature festival run by *The Times*, a tour of British libraries, and a string of published work in *Cotswold Life* magazine lasting eight years – each one would help fund another happy family getaway with my Dad in our small touring caravan.

Mum not only wrote autobiographical tales, but fiction, poetry, songs, musicals, technical workbooks and factual articles – as a child it was not uncommon for me to see her work in glossy magazines, newspapers, on BBC and ITV, to hear it played on the radio, or performed live. Unlike her Dad, she was a "Mum of *Many* Words" – and countless people have enjoyed them. This certainly inspired my own work in the media: acting, directing, animating, and writing films, books, comics and music.

I never got to meet her father – sadly he passed away just before I was born. When Mum told him that she thought she was pregnant, some of the last of his "few" words were "Nothing would make me happier". I wish we would have had a chance to meet, but everything that Mum told me about him over the years made me admire him greatly. When my agent told me that for professional purposes I would need to change my surname, I chose to repurpose my middle one, "Victor".

Growing up, we weren't rich, we weren't from London, we didn't have celebrity connections, but I watched Mum get success by just being creative and not being afraid to put herself out there – following her example has been the blueprint for my own career. She often donates profits from her ventures to charities and good causes, another great example that I follow. One area where we differ is that while I'm happy to shout about my achievements to all who will listen, Mum humbly downplays her talents. It's taken much persuading, but I'm so happy to have been able to help her get not one, but *four* full books published spanning her forty year career, preserved so that she will inspire people for generations to come, just as she's always done for me.

ABOUT THE AUTHOR

Ann Leyfield is a renowned writer whose work in poetry, prose and song have been regularly featured in British media since the 1980s (as Ann Jones), spanning television, radio, newspapers, books and magazines. A four-time selection for *The Times* and *The Sunday Times* Cheltenham Literature Festival through *Gloucestershire Writers' Network*, Ann also created the worldwide best-selling factual series of *Cracking the Code* books, several well loved children's musicals and her acclaimed autobiography *A Wealth of Pennies* was first published through the *Daily Mail*.

ALSO FROM THE AUTHOR
Further publications in this series, from Victorious MCG

A WEALTH OF PENNIES
An Autobiography of a Child of the Fifties
ISBN: 9798873594504

EVERY POEM HAS A STORY
Snapshots of a Lifetime Distilled into Verse
ISBN: 9798872897187

SONGS TO MAKE A DIFFERENCE
Christian Songs and the Stories That Gave Them Life
ISBN: 9798873597192

Available worldwide on Amazon, Kindle, Audible, and independent retail outlets.

Printed in Great Britain
by Amazon